IRIDESCENT LUST

MEN OF VANGUARD BOOK 3

RYDER O'MALLEY

MEN OF VANGUARD SERIES

MEN OF VANGUARD

Irresistible Power Prequel

(Patreon Exclusive Novella)

Infamous Heart

Infernal Justice

Iridescent Lust

Invincible Nemesis

ACKNOWLEDGMENTS

Thank you my Patreon Supporters

Miranda Dal Zovo

James Holcomb

Emily S. Hurricane

Jason Janes

1

———————

"… AND THAT'S WHY I'LL NEVER SLEEP WITH A MAN WHO CAN clone himself again."

I was halfway done with my apple juice before I realized the three of them were frozen in place. Griffin's jaw was hanging open wide enough I could tell he made Sebastian a happy man. Xander, on the other hand, didn't believe me. If his eyebrow could move any higher up his face, he'd be wearing it as a toupee. But it was Bernard who maintained a poker face. Thankfully, his rapid blinking served as morse code, spelling out, "Alejandro, I'm proud of you." Or at least that's the lie I'd tell myself.

"What?" I asked, taking a bite of my eggs. "Lube is expensive."

At any other coffee shop, detailing the events of my bedroom would be considered poor form, but not at the

HideOut. I have no idea why this served as our base of operations. Something tells me Bernard had something to do with it. Once the rest of us passed the initiation, we joined the breakfast club. In the Ward, it was known as the gay-friendly place to get your morning caffeine buzz.

The owner, Chad, leaned over my shoulder, carefully pouring coffee into my cup. "Alejandro, I have no idea how you're still upright."

"Only time he's not on his back," Xander chimed in.

I glared at the brute before kicking him under the table. The paramedic puckered his lips and blew me a kiss. All was forgiven, for now.

"Or on all fours," Griffin added. Great, they're all going to take a turn.

All eyes turned to Bernard, waiting for his comment. I'll admit, the daddy bear always had a good zinger. He had this knack for holding his tongue and then waiting for the least suspecting moment before he stopped us in our tracks.

"Don't look at me," he said before sipping from his coffee. "I'm still trying to figure out how triple penetration is even possible."

"Chad, get me a napkin and a pen. I'll draw you a diagram."

The barista was gone before I could swipe his notepad. If it wasn't so busy, I'd have Xander and Griffin help me put on a demonstration. As I counted the sugar containers on the table, I froze, eyeing the big man. He might serve as the father figure of this quartet, but I'd never consider Bernard a prude.

"Wait…" I made sure the grin was visible to everybody. "You know."

"Know what?" He took another sip, eyes never making contact.

"You know." That dirty man. I was almost proud.

"Bernard hasn't had sex this century. Leave the man alone," Xander said.

"I assumed he was celibate," Griffin chimed in.

"I'm right here." If Bernard was our father figure, we were triplets out of control. It meant breakfast was never boring.

Like always, the coffee shop was packed with patrons, and only a couple seats remained free as people guzzled coffee. At one of the long tables, half a dozen men sat with laptops open, treating the HideOut as their personal office. Overall, the vibe remained relaxed as Chad worked behind the counter, steaming milk for a man.

"Is the Alley picking back up?" Griffin asked, attempting to have a genuine conversation. I suppose I could round myself out and have a bit of depth.

"It's picked up, but nowhere near the popularity from before. It's almost like the heroes are a little less flashy since the depowering." I could live with a slow workday, but my wallet didn't enjoy missing out on tips. It was also messing with my extracurricular activities in the bedroom. Neither of those things made me a cheerful man.

"I bet they're a bit shaken," Bernard said. He wiped the dribble of coffee from his perfectly sculpted beard. If he wasn't the patriarch of this breakfast cult, I'd have taken a stab at him. I'd have to ask Xander if he ever got the man naked while they were dating. I had questions that needed measurements.

"Aliens invade Earth. They all get together and beat up the bad guys. This was waking up one morning to find out they were helpless civilians. That must have shaken their confidence."

Bernard's eyes glazed over into that thousand-yard stare, where it's obvious he's processing his own words. Once he takes another sip of coffee, he wipes off his mustache. Damn, he was the one man who could pull it off and still be sexy as hell.

Griffin bumped my leg. It was the cue to not dig into the conversation any deeper. Bernard might think he was being subtle, but Griff and I knew his secret. He was the legendary Sentinel, a member of the Centurions. We pretended we didn't know, but if he thought a mask was hiding his rugged jaw and fierce eyes, he was a fool. For now, I nodded, and Griffin put down the fork he prepared to drive into my thigh like a good friend.

I hung out with crazy people, crazy loyal, but still crazy. I held up the spoon used to stir cream in my coffee to inspect my beard. Running my hand over the dark hair, it felt as if there were only a few days before I needed to return to the barber. This mug made me money at the bar. I couldn't look like I lived on the street. A tight shave would have just the right amount of black stubble peppering my face. Rugged, I liked to think it was the perfect word to describe me. I set the spoon down, not wanting them to consider me vain.

"I never thought I'd say it, but I'm glad the heroes are back." In a world with superheroes, Xander opposed their existence for as long as I knew. After he met Aiden, his attitude shifted. I wanted to ask if Aiden was a member of the caped community, but I assumed it was a faux pas to out a hero.

"Speaking of heroes..." Griffin started.

"You're going to start wearing spandex?" Xander interjected.

"He saves that for the bedroom," I said as I fist-bumped Xander. If we didn't love one another, we'd be cited for harassment.

"I'd subscribe to that OnlyFans page."

If I had just said that, it'd have been teasing. But as Bernard mumbled the words with a straight face, the rest of us broke into laughter. This breakfast was the perfect end to a long night at the bar.

"No, I save that for the bedroom. And, no, I have good news about Sebastian. It appears that Mr. Bossman—"

"Can we take a moment to discuss the name?"

I waited for one of them to pile on the comments. But neither Xander nor Bernard spoke. Really? Was I the only one who found it ironic that Griffin's boss was named Bossman? I questioned our friendship.

"He's taking a less active role in the magazine. Since Damien Vex tried to poach one of his employees, Bossman returned the favor. Sebastian is the new bossman."

Griffin worked for a superhero magazine, and after some drama with the local competition, they stepped up and promoted him. Meanwhile, his boyfriend worked for their rival, and yet somehow, they maintained a picture-perfect relationship.

"Congrats." Bernard held up his coffee in a salute. "It's good to get him out of there. Now, for Aiden."

Xander's boyfriend worked at the rival magazine. Was there something in the water cooler over there I needed to check out? Maybe if I hung out at the entrance, I'd find myself a bearish man to bring home. It appeared they were a dime a dozen.

"That's not it." Griffin's excitement oozed from every word.

"Your pregnant?" Xander asked.

"No." Griffin gave him the finger.

"Not for their lack of trying," Bernard snickered.

"I hate you all." Griffin tried to look irked, but the smile persevered. I finished the last of my eggs and drained the cup of coffee. I probably shouldn't drink this much, but I would not make it to the end of the conversation without a boost of caffeine. My bed was calling to me.

"Since he's going to be working in the Ward. He's decided to move in."

I choked on my coffee. "Whoa. Moving in? That's a big step, like masivo."

"I think we're there. We've been talking about it for a while, but it just didn't make sense working on opposite sides of the city. Now, we'll be able to walk to work."

Work. Commute. Home. I was struggling to see how any two people could tolerate being around each other that much. While Bernard and Xander congratulated the man, it felt as if the walls were closing in. Somebody in my space all day, every day?

"Won't you get tired of each other?" Oh. I didn't mean to say that part out loud.

"What? No?" Griffin spat back.

Bernard kicked me under the table. I'm pretty sure Xander did the same. "I mean, that's going from seeing each other in the evenings to all day. Every day. I can't imagine being around anybody—"

Kicking hadn't worked, so Bernard leaned forward, clutching my leg under the table. I stopped as his fingers drilled into my thigh, threatening to leave bruises. I wasn't trying to rain on Griffin's parade. He found something that worked for him and Sebastian. But me? That type of commitment might very well be my kryptonite.

"We're happy for you, Griff. Aren't we, Alejandro?" Bernard's smile might be saying one thing, but the side-eye was telling a different story.

"Whatever works for you and that studly man. I'm happy for you, Griffin."

"Ditto. But isn't your apartment small?" Xander asked.

"Oh,"—Griffin was like a kid in a candy store. I'm not sure I could handle this level of excitement as I fought off drooping eyelids. Chad was going to need to just pour the pot in my mouth at this rate—"With two incomes, we'll find a much nicer place in the Ward."

Before we could continue the congratulations, the entire cafe went silent. The sudden change in volume, coupled with the vibration in my pocket, could only mean one thing, the HeroApp™. Vanguard City's personal app used to help citizens keep track of the diabolical villains that gravitated to our city. With our plethora of heroes, I never understood why the bad guys didn't find a nice rural town to lord over. But as everybody scanned their cell phones, it was obvious a superhero battle was imminent.

Both Xander and Bernard jumped to their feet. Bernard needed to go find his supersuit and squeeze those beefy thighs into the form-fitting fabric, and Xander rescued fallen superheroes as a paramedic. They'd be off to do their part to save the world. For me, if it was a big enough battle and the heroes won, it meant the club would bustle this evening. Good, I needed a full tip jar.

Xander and Bernard bolted for the door without so much as a farewell. I turned to Griffin, who was rolling his eyes back in his head. "I swear they do this just so we have to pick up the tab."

Dammit, he was right. As I fished out my wallet, I apologized for being a downer. "I don't want you to think I'm not happy for you and Sebastian. You two are perfect together."

"Thanks. Eventually, you'll find somebody."

He meant well, but it wasn't like I was looking to settle down. There were too many superheroes with bulging muscles I had yet to see naked. I smiled as we tossed money down on the table.

Try as he might, I couldn't imagine one man being my everything.

2

There was no point in trying to be tidy. The clothes came off the moment I shut the door. It was long past my bedtime, and all I wanted was a shower and to curl up in bed. To think, I had considered taking one of the heroes up on their offer for a wild time. Thankfully, my better judgment overrode my cock. Falling asleep in the middle of sex left the wrong impression.

I paused in the living room. I needed to answer the toughest question of the evening. To the right, a doorway to the bedroom, or left, one leading to the shower. There might as well have been a black hole originating from my bed, determined to draw me into its gravity. It was sheer stubbornness that pushed me to the bathroom.

"You'll thank me when you don't wake up smelling like vodka."

I had spent the better part of a decade making a name for myself at the Alley. Being the best bartender at the club meant they asked for me by name. I might pour a mean cocktail, but it was the personality that kept them coming back. It didn't hurt that I was catering to the superhero elite of Vanguard City.

What I hadn't known was that superheroes were a bit more open-minded than most. It started with a bit of shameless flirting. Apparently, being adored came with the cape, and they ate it up. I noticed the tip jar gain momentum, so I continued to push boundaries. Flirting turned to innuendo, and more than one hero made it abundantly clear that they were interested.

I spin the handle to the shower. While it reached scalding temperatures, I did a quick inspection of my beard. The usual stubble had gotten longer than I cared for, but I was too tired to break out the trimmers. The only items on my itinerary were shower and then bed.

I stepped into the shower, turning so the pulsating stream could pound away at the space between my shoulders. With one long sigh, the tension eased through my shoulders. I had my choice of bedrooms for this evening, but once in a while, the only one that mattered was mine. Sometimes you need to shower alone. I know, the revelation shocked me too.

My cock jumped at the thought of showering with another man. That's how my reputation went from being the best bartender at Midnight Alley to being the resident "hero chaser." It all started with Trident, one of the most well-known heroes in all of Vanguard. I thought it was a joke that he slipped me his number, but when I got off work and texted him, he was just finishing up a combat situation against the Lizard King. He wanted to celebrate a victory and when he sent a photo in only his briefs, I knew there'd be no going back.

I lathered up, washing off the grime. Not so different from the way he had done it. The only difference was that Trident could control water, and he had skillfully directed the stream around my body. I like to think I'm plenty creative in the bedroom, but nothing prepared me for a supernatural romp. Once the soap washed away, he reposi-tioned the water until he cascaded toward my groin, split-ting just before touching my cock. Trident had my attention before he used the water to tease.

Daydreaming in the shower led my cock into wanting attention. The last coffee was already wearing off, and I could have leaned against the glass wall and closed my eyes.

"Sorry, buddy." Yes, it was perfectly acceptable to talk to your penis. I'd fight anybody who argued. "Maybe tomor-row. Wouldn't want to fall asleep on you."

The bathroom grew silent as I shut off the water. Toweling off, I tossed it on the sink and wandered into the living room. The couch called to me, begging me to rest my head. It was tempting, but my back would hate me when I woke up in the afternoon. No, I needed to pass out in my bed before the sun rose.

As I passed through the living room, I pulled the cord on the shades, leaving my apartment in darkness. The one downside to sleeping through the morning was that the sun refused to cut me a break.

"Stupid sun," I grumbled.

In the bedroom, I collapsed onto the bed, my face sinking into the pillow. It'd only be a minute before I was out cold. I reached out to the empty side of the bed, hunting. My head shot up when I couldn't find my furry companion.

"Where'd you go?"

Scooting across the bed, I reached for the floor, fishing around. My fingers grazed the soft fur of my bedtime buddy. I grabbed the arm of my stuffed bear and pulled him onto the bed.

"Mi amado."

I wrapped my arm around the gray stuffed animal, clinging to him as if he were a real burly bear. Unlike the many men who temporarily occupied the empty pillows next to mine, I never had to worry about Amado vanishing in the morning.

Nuzzling my face into the back of his head, I closed my eyes. His fur tickled my nose, and for a moment, I thought I might sneeze. Before I could brush the fuzz away...

3

A COOL BREEZE WHIPPED THROUGH THE WARD, MAKING FOR a pleasant sunset. There were many parts of my day when I stopped and had to soak in the beauty. But watching as the sun turn shades of orange, its fading rays covering the brownstone buildings, was always my favorite. I slowed my walk, admiring the many people on the sidewalk pausing to soak in the beauty.

It was weird working the night shift. As the rest of the world settled in, preparing to wind down, I had barely started. I wouldn't call myself a night owl, often fighting to keep my eyes open by the end of the night. But it did always leave me out of time with the rest of the world. My dinner was Griffin's breakfast. My bedtime served as Bernard's lunch break. While they crawled into their beds, I was busy slinging drinks.

We occupied a different world. The barracks, the waitresses, we'd collect at late night diners and meet with the hotel staff, the sex workers, and more than a few drug dealers. We were the exhausted people who shuffled through the day, failing to be children of the day. I got older, and it seemed everybody else in the industry stayed the same age. Somewhere along the line, I outgrew the perpetual parties.

Then I became a bartender at the Alley. I wasn't interested in meeting up with coworkers after we closed shop. Unlike any job before, I was captivated by the superheroes that walked through the doors, each one acting like they were a champion. There weren't many who saved the world on the daily, but even rescuing a cat from a tree had them puffing out their chests like they prevented a mass extinction event.

And the sex.

I let out a sigh. It might be the fact they understood hiding a part of themselves from the world, or perhaps they were beyond labels. Either way, I found that sexuality amongst heroes was a bit more flexible than the rest of the population. They might present as straight for the news crews, but between the sheets, I found they were less rigid about their identities. Much like Vanguard, I had more than my share of heroes.

I snickered at the idea of becoming a hero chaser.

"Help!" It wouldn't be a Tuesday without a Vanguard

citizen being kidnapped by a villain mastermind. "Somebody, help me."

I turned toward the source of the voice. The alley was clad in shadows, tall buildings on either side protecting it from the rays of the setting sun. A bit of trash rolled about in the grim space. I could swear that the narrow street was desaturated, as if something had siphoned away the color.

"Really?" I eyed the street, heading to the club. It glowed a vibrant orange, basking in the light. There was a richness, and I swear I could hear birds chirping off in the distance. Was that the sound of an ice cream truck? Everything to my right was picturesque and deserving of a painting. The alley, however, screamed, "Danger ahead."

"What could go wrong?" And with those magic words, I ensured that I'd be taken hostage, or vaporized, or worse yet, had to listen to a villain monologue. I might as well be a busty blonde running in high heels. The made-for-TV movie wrote itself.

"Is there anybody down there?" I stepped forward until my toes rested on the line where the majestic street turned into the gray alley of despair. "If you're going to kill me, you have to tell me now. It's a rule." I'm sure there were meetings at villain central where they discussed what was and wasn't considered fair. Did they operate by a governing code of conduct? I'd need to ask Bernard all these questions when he came out from behind the mask.

"Help." It sounded like a basic damsel-in-distress cry.

"It's been months since I was last kidnapped." I stepped over the threshold, leaving the safety of the street. "Are you there? What's wrong?"

A large trash can in the alley rattled. I froze, expecting a man wearing his underwear on the outside of his pants to yell, "Gotcha!" A second later, I could see a delicate hand spill out from behind the trashcan. There were no more cries, just a woman's arm.

"Can I help?" There was no answer. This was a trap. I should have known better. They taught us to avoid these situations in grade school. According to Mrs. Bradley, I should turn around and run until I found a grown-up. Unfortunately, I had been held back that year. I'd show that vile woman I wasn't scared. I couldn't *not* help, but the tightening in my stomach should have been all the convincing I needed to run away.

"Let me help..." The woman's arm connected to a beautiful naked torso. She was downright stunning until the scales started around her navel. From there downward, her body elongated into what I could only describe as a snake. Yup, I had found a Gorgon. "Dammit, I can hear Mrs. Bradley with her 'I told you so.'"

There was no point in running. She grew twice my height, suspended by the muscles in her serpentine torso. Once she opened her eyes, I could see the yellow in her iris'. I had walked into a dark alley expecting something other than a giant snake woman growing taller as she debated eating me. Serves me right. Before bed tonight, I'd see if Mrs. Bradley was still alive. Then I'd write her the longest apology note.

"I don't suppose you're just hanging out? You know, maybe you're just trying to scare somebody? Oh, no! See, I'm scared. Now, I'm just going to head on my way."

"I'm so hungry."

"I'm high in cholesterol. You should find yourself a vegan. I'll see if there are any roaming the street."

I turned around to see the tail end of the woman's body blocking my escape. Great, this was going to make me late for work. You'd think with all the bad guys robbing banks or destroying apartment buildings, employers would be more forgiving. Nope, we still got docked for coming in late.

I could send out an alert on the HeroApp™. It would be just a matter of staying alive until somebody swooped in and carried me to safety. I moved my hand toward my pocket, but before I could slip it inside, the woman's tail flicked my hand.

"So hungry."

Somewhere off in the distance, it sounded as if somebody whistled. Not a song, just one long note, as if they couldn't carry a tune. It got louder and, as I looked over my shoulder, I expected to see a man walk past the mouth of the alley.

The crash had me spinning around to face the woman and, at the same time, jumping back as if a bomb had gone off. The sound of metal and asphalt hitting the building walls made me shield my face. I landed on the ground, curling into a ball, hoping that I survived the fallout.

I spread my fingers to see the damage and found myself inches away from a pair of boots. Past them, a car had fallen from the sky, landing on the woman, burying her under a heap of metallic rubble.

I turned to the legs, following up the contours of their owner's body, only pausing for a moment at the man's crotch before taking in his chest. Magenta and black brand colors made up most of his costume. The torso appeared to be covered in triangle mirrors. I didn't recognize him, but at this point, I couldn't keep up with the sheer volume of people gifted with powers.

Holding out his hand, he spoke in a flat tone. "Come with me if you want to live."

I raised an eyebrow as I brushed the bits of asphalt from my goatee. "Thanks, but I'm good. I'm just going—"

"Really? I just saved your life and delivered an epic one-liner, and you're going to say no?"

"Epic? You stole your dialogue."

"Harsh. You can't leave me hanging, man."

I chuckled at his insistence. At any moment, I expected him to pout and stomp his feet. They trained superheroes to save the victim. They didn't know how to handle a victim willing to save themselves.

I should have walked away, but I couldn't help but stare at the full beard wrapping around his chin. His chest was wide enough, so I wasn't sure I could reach around him with my arms. This husky do-gooder wanted to save me. Perhaps I should think of it as more of an opportunity and less of an annoyance.

"Are you going to sulk if I say no?"

"Dude, the rest of the heroes at central command would make so much fun of me. You don't want to be why my photo winds up on the wall of shame." Did he just bat his eyes at me? Was I being seduced into being rescued?

The car groaned as the woman freed herself. Her scream filled the alley, and whatever was about to happen between this hero and his foe, I didn't want to be present. I reached out, grabbed his hand and with a swift jerk, he pulled me to my feet.

"Fine, you can save me."

He wrapped his arm around my waist, pulling me tightly against his body. Any protests I had vanished as his hand rested in the small of my back. With only inches between our faces, I resisted the urge to kiss him. If I made it out alive, *then* he'd get to kiss the damsel in distress. Right now, I wasn't entirely sure he—

Leaning backward, he dragged me along, and I tensed, preparing to thump against the pavement again. Despite falling, there was no impact. I opened my eyes to see we were standing upright amidst a strong breeze.

"Where are..." Somehow, we were standing on top of one of the taller buildings in the Ward. Behind my savior, a ring of glowing light revealed an image of the alley. Teleportation. That was a new one for me. My mind went to the gutter, trying to imagine how that could turn into a fun time in the bedroom.

"Hate to save and scurry, but I should finish beating her to a pulp."

I was about to protest when he fell downward. I looked to the rooftop to see another circular portal where he had been standing. He had teleported himself back into the alley to stop the woman. Before I could argue, both portals shut, and I was left alone.

"Well, at least I'm alive."

I made my way to the door leading to the stairs down through the building. As I tugged on the handle, it refused to open. I pulled with all my might, but it wasn't enough to pry the door open. In a fit of rage, I pounded on the metal before giving it a swift kick.

"Alive," I grumbled, "and late for work."

"How the hell is 'thick with a body I want climbing on top of me' not a valid description? ¡No mames!"

Griffin was the last person I dared call to tell them someone trapped me on a roof. Bernard hadn't picked up his phone and Xander must be on a call. They'd have been more practical in their advice of getting free. But no, I got stuck with Griffin, who only cared about identifying the superhero who abandoned me on the roof.

"Nope. I checked, nobody listed as 'Hero Alejandro wants to bang.' How did you wind up on the roof, anyway? Is this going to be some weird sex thing?"

I needed to work on my reputation. Or maybe I just needed to stop telling them all the times I couldn't wait until I got home to undress a hero. "He teleported me up here. He was trying to get me away from the snake woman."

"Female snake? Or half snake, half woman?"

"The second."

"Nagatine. That's an easy one."

"You're lucky Sebastian thinks you're cute."

I banged the back of my head against the door again. In the movies, there would be a broom or metal pole I could use to pry the door open. How come I was on the cleanest roof in all of Vanguard City?

I'm sure Scarlet would understand. Everybody at the club had been kidnapped at least once since working there. I'm not sure if the Villain Pay Protection act would extend to being rescued by a hero. Great, another night of crappy pay.

I'd play his game. "Broad. Teleporter. Suit was dark

pants, impressive bulge. The chest was like mirrors, I think?"

"Locator?"

I shook my head. "No, he had both arms."

"Shifter?"

"Nope. He didn't blink in and out. It was more like a portal."

"Oh, maybe he's in the portal category."

Really? Were there that many heroes that they had to differentiate between teleport and portal? I almost said something, but I remembered two women arguing about the technical aspects of their power. One could summon fire, and the other made objects combust and created fire. Both were fire-wielding heroes, but to them, they might as well have been from different planets. Ironic, because neither of them was from Earth.

"Was he hot?"

There were several ways to reach the definition of hot. The most obvious is, were they the perfect blend of muscle and soft padding? I preferred the term huskular, but I'd also check out a guy who identified as a dad bod, chunky, chubby, bearish, or even barrel-chested. I needed a bit of charm, the ability to converse with a bit of sass. Lastly, was the good-guy meter. A bad boy might get my attention for a moment, but I didn't need trouble. I could find that all on my own. Husky, charming, and a good guy. Dammit, he was hot.

"Very hot."

Griffin went silent for a few seconds. "My hot, or your hot?"

"Whoa, shots fired."

"I'm not one to judge."

I brought the phone close to my lips. "Griffin Smith, I am going to reach through this phone and strangle you."

There was a long pause before I growled. "He was *hot*."

"EO."

"Excuse me?"

"That's the teleporter's name. Unless you're into the busty ladies."

I might be down for some unusual bedroom activities, but they all required a penis. I bet EO's package was impressive out of his suit. He didn't strike me as a hero who wore an athletic cup to increase their underwear profile. The more I thought about it, the further into the fantasy of his rescue I fell.

"Alejandro, come back to me."

"Sorry, I was daydreaming."

"Any luck getting off the roof?" Now that he had solved the riddle, Griffin could focus on the actual issue at hand.

"There's nothing up here. I already threw myself against the door once. It's not budging. You're going to need to come and rescue me."

The sun was nearly gone now and the city lights had come to life. It was going to be a cold evening if I couldn't get down from here. I hated to make him travel across the city, but it looked like my hero wasn't returning to sweep me off my feet.

"Did you look for a key?"

"It's not like there's a key in the handle."

"Writers go on the roof of the Beacon all the time to smoke. Check around the top of the door."

I leaned my head back, annoyed at the possibility of such a straightforward solution. It was hard to see in the dim light, but the door had a thick frame around it. I rolled over and clamored to my feet before running my fingers along the top. I froze as I grazed something.

"Dammit."

"No luck?" Griffin asked.

"Not that. You were right." The key in front of my face was barely visible. I had to resist the urge to hurl it off the side of the building. I could have been on my way to work if I had used my head instead of trying to bust the door down. Okay, perhaps calling Griffin hadn't been a complete waste.

"You'll be picking up my tab at breakfast."

I growled. "Fine."

"Have a good night at work." Before I could offer a snotty reply, he'd hung up. Sometimes I wanted to slap him. Okay, truth be told, I always wanted to slap him, but I'd consider him the second hero to save me tonight.

I unlocked the door and with a grinding pull, I could

see the stairwell leading down. With a quick glance over the shoulder, it made me sad EO hadn't returned to whisk me away. I'd peel the suit off his body. It was the right thing to do after he risked his life to protect me. Maybe someday I'd get to return the favor.

For now, work called.

4

———

"Staff meeting in five." The voice boomed over the sound system as if God himself was speaking to us. I had barely started in on cutting limes for the night. If I didn't get the bar set up, drinks would be slow, and nobody liked to wait for their signature cocktail.

"¡Oye! Being kidnapped is now the second worst part of my night. What's this about?" I asked Bruno.

He gave a shrug as he approached the bar. It was almost comical that Midnight Alley kept a bouncer in the front of the club. Bruno had biceps thicker than my neck, but none of that could compete with a person capable of shooting lasers out of their eyes. His charisma bordered on the supernatural. More than once, I questioned if he had powers of his own.

He finished aligning the chairs against the bar,

making sure he turned each at a forty-five-degree angle. Going through the checklist was cathartic, like we were soldiers preparing for the onslaught of war. Each night, we battled as a DJ or band filled the space with music. Once the patrons arrived, we'd be called to arms, and it'd be non-stop until the sun threatened to break the horizon.

"No clue. Do you need help?" He leaned over the counter and grabbed a stack of lemons and a knife. The cuts weren't pretty, but I wouldn't argue with the help.

"Scarlet never calls meetings," he said.

"Right? Who wants to deal with us with the lights on?"

The club had once been derelict, dangerously close to being condemned and bulldozed by the city. Scarlet sank every penny she had into turning it into a bar influenced by the speakeasies from prohibition with a healthy dose of art déco decor. The bar had been about to sink when she cashed in on our connection to the superhero community. Overnight, the bar turned into a success, with lines wrapping around the block. Midnight Alley had become a hot spot that continued to trend on social media, all thanks to a former superhero's vision.

"Maybe we're all getting raises?" Bruno waited until I locked eyes with him before he laughed. She was an amazing boss, and often we made outstanding money, but she made sure we busted our butts to earn it.

"Last time we had a staff meeting was when the superheroes faced their counterparts from the mirror dimension?"

I laughed. "Oh yeah, I remember that. It was standing room only, and boy, did they want to keep the booze flowing."

"Didn't you go home with that guy in the armor?"

Bruno was well aware of my reputation for chasing capes. "That guy? You mean those guys? Was standing room only in my bedroom too."

"I wish I was gay," he laughed. "I wouldn't mind a superhero lady friend, but they never seem interested in lil' ol' me."

"If you were gay, I'd be on my knees in the front of that line." I blew him a kiss to accentuate the point. He blushed, which only made him more adorable.

The other bartenders cracked up at our exchange. They were amused by my suave moves behind the counter. They were just as bad. Midnight Alley hired a particular type, and thankfully, this meant we were ready to schmooze with the clients, with or without our pants.

"Listen up," Scarlet's voice struck a chord somewhere in the base of the brain, and everybody froze. "Sorry about that." Every time she turned assertive, she reverted to her siren ways, barking commands that men couldn't resist. After years of being in the field, she rarely lost control. This could only mean the staff meeting had unnerved her.

"There's no easy way to say this..." Would Scarlet

declare the bartenders could no longer drink with the patrons? Was she about to cap how many comp drinks we could give? Worse yet, was she going to say we weren't allowed to fraternize with the heroes? My sex life would come to an abrupt stop.

"I've decided to retire and sell the club."

Okay, so there *was* something worse. The waiters were abuzz, quick to discuss their job prospects. The talent manager, DJ, and security staff held still, refusing to partake in idle gossip. I could probably get another job bartending at one of the other high-society clubs. Truth was, I didn't want another job. Midnight Alley had become a bright spot in an otherwise boring life.

Scarlet brushed neon blue hair behind her ear, showing off the dangling jewelry. It hadn't been a statement she took lightly. Of all the employees, she might be the only person who loved the club more than me. This announcement took its toll. She dabbed her eyes with a white cloth, careful not to smear her immaculate makeup.

"Somebody is exploring the possibility of buying the club and keeping it open."

The waiters let out a sigh of relief. For them, this was a job, a paycheck they could depend on every Friday night. Without Scarlet circulating the club, I didn't have faith it'd survive to the end of the year.

"Why?" I asked.

She moved toward the grand piano pushed to the side

of the club. No matter where she stood, even amongst the dark red walls and gold accents, Scarlet commanded the room. It wasn't her abilities that made her formidable. Her tenacity as a businesswoman made her a storm. On the nights we transformed the club into a speakeasy, she'd sit atop the piano, serenading the room. Scarlet and Midnight Alley were one and the same. Now she was leaving us.

"Long ago, I made a promise to Max we'd see the world. It's time."

"So you're abandoning us?"

Bruno grabbed my forearm, digging his fingers into my flesh. When I tried to pull away, he held fast, and the moment I caught his eye, I could see the warning. With a quick nod of the chin, Scarlet sobbed. I knew better. There were two things she loved: Max and Midnight Alley.

"Go."

Barely audible, her command rippled through the room. Without unleashing the full might of her voice, we were aware of the manipulation. Bruno released my arm, leaving me to return to the bar. Before I started on the limes, I regretted speaking out in front of the staff. Even if I felt she was ditching us for greener pastures, Scarlet deserved more respect.

I wanted to apologize, but the echo of her command wouldn't let me leave my station.

The bar backs danced around me, polishing glasses, ensuring the presentation met the owner's strict guidelines.

Scarlet pressed keys on the piano, humming along to a melody that never quite reached her fingertips.

She spun about, meandering toward the bar. I half expected her to reach across the counter and slap me. The mascara had run down her cheeks, making it look as if her tears were black. Superpowers were the least impressive thing about her as she pulled back her shoulders, finding her stride.

"Buy the club."

The knife slipped through the lime, butchering the fruit. Her voice wavered with the statement, a sign she spoke without her hypnotic powers. She reached out until her hand slid over mine.

"Buy it, Alejandro."

"But you said—"

"I haven't agreed to the sale. This has been my life for such a long time. I met Max here. He would come and listen to me sing before the supers. As I finished my set, he always gave me a nod. If I didn't approach him, he wouldn't have talked to me. We closed the bar that night talking about dreams. He doesn't believe me, but I knew then that I'd marry him."

The confident businesswoman had a soft side that few saw. Out of all her employees, I had known her the longest, and somewhere along the way, she stopped being my boss and became part of my extended family. When she gave birth to her daughter, I was the one who drove Max to the hospital.

"I wouldn't know the first thing—"

"Don't kid yourself. There is nobody here more passionate about the Alley. If we didn't need the money to retire, I'd simply sign it over." She gripped my hand, squeezing my fingers. "You're the only person who loves it as much as me."

"Is this going to be an awkward three-way?"

She laughed. "When has a three-way ever been awkward for the legendary Alejandro?"

"But the buyer?"

"There's time." She let go and walked away. With a slight turn of her head, she eyed me over her shoulder. "Kid, I wish you would see yourself the way I do. You might not know it, but you're ready for more."

Scarlet had dropped a bomb before walking away. My cheeks grew hot, and in a well-rehearsed motion, I grabbed the tequila from under the bar. I flipped over a shot glass, filled it, and slammed the drink. Repeat. Three shots later, liquid courage coursed through my veins.

"Define *more*, Scarlet."

Flare wasn't required, but it was appreciated. Sure, I could throw a little muscle into shaking the woman's cocktail and it'd be a fine drink. But adding my signature shake of the hips while vodka sloshes in the mixer ensures a bigger tip. It's accented as I open it, giving a lengthy pour and an extra olive on the toothpick.

Raven smiled as I slapped down a napkin, setting her drink down in front of her. Like always, she takes a sip, taking a moment to savor the drink before she nods her approval. "Your martini is the perfect end to a day of protecting the museum's jewels from thieves."

"And yet you're stealing my heart," I shouted over the music.

With black eyes, I couldn't be sure if they rolled back, but I had my suspicions. "When you decide to play for the other team, call me." She slid the money across the table. "Keep it."

The tip jar had a ways to go before it reached pre-depowering numbers, but it just meant I had to dial up the charm. The crowd inside continued to grow, but there weren't many heavy hitters from the superhero community. As I searched for familiar masks, I found most of the Alley's patrons were new supers. It was good to get fresh blood, but we always hoped for one of the billionaire heroes like the Machinist to come in and throw money around.

As Raven turned toward the table with her feathered husband, Raven froze. I followed her eyes to the door. "¡Por Dios! There goes the night."

The Guild, five of the most egotistical supers roaming

Vanguard City. On multiple occasions, their leader went toe-to-toe with Scarlet. Eclipse acted as if they were on par with the Centurions, but to date, nobody had seen them saving the city. There were plenty of people with superpowers that frequented the club who didn't use their abilities to protect the average Joe, but none of them bragged about their superiority. No, Eclipse needed a seat for him and an entire table for his ego.

He also didn't understand the concept of tipping.

Eclipse and his lackeys wore tailored white suits that accentuated their muscles. The cowl covering the Guild leader's face made it impossible to identify the jerk underneath, but I assumed he was nothing to look at. Heroes who padded their suits always had something to hide alongside their alter ego. With the bulge in his suit, I suspected he'd be neither a shower nor a grower.

Of course, he headed straight for the bar.

"Whisky, top-shelf, heavy on the pour."

Translated to refined but smug, and I don't know the name of what I like to drink, but I want people to know I'm worth it. Heavy on the pour was patron speak, for I want two drinks for the price of one. Don't piss off your bartender. We have our own superpowers.

Sitting amongst the top-shelf booze are bottles of house liquor, decoys for our problem customers. I grab a bottom-of-the-barrel whisky and pour freely. It tastes like ass, but this man wouldn't know quality alcohol. I toss in a couple of ice cubes to add insult to injury. I repeat, don't piss off your bartender.

"Enjoy." No flare, no effort. The man deserved less, but Scarlet would have my head if I spat in his drink.

"Any big players tonight?" Even his voice was harsh, like he's using a modulator to make it extra gravely. I'd bet when he gained his powers, he watched superhero movies and took notes.

"Just the usual patrons." I might chase heroes into the bedroom, but this guy wanted to find the most well-known hero for fame by association. For a man with no reputation, he wanted to climb the ranks with the least amount of work. I wasn't going to help him.

"You know some of the big names in the game? You'll have to introduce me."

His cronies stood at his back, surveying the club. Three men and a woman acted less like a team and more like accessories. None of them ordered drinks, so they weren't my problem. Scarlet would be proud of how I held my tongue. They needed to leave before my resolve faded.

"I know you *know* plenty of heroes..." Was I about to get slut shamed by a man who hadn't had his penis played with by another person in a decade? So what if he had mystical abilities? The bile rose as I prepared to hurl a string of insults that'd leave him scraping his ego off the floor.

"Why don't you—"

The portal opened to the side of Eclipse. EO stepped through. "You would not believe how hard it is to keep a snake woman in prison. I couldn't finish the paperwork before an officer screamed about her slithering away."

The moment Eclipse saw the fluids on EO's body armor, he stepped away. Heaven forbid his immaculate suit got any amount of wear. I handed EO a towel from behind the bar. He did his best to clean up, but he'd need a shower before he got all the gunk off his suit. He dropped the towel, and it vanished through a portal to some unknown location.

"You definitely don't want that."

After rescuing me, I was glad to see EO emerge victorious. But the grin stretching across my face was thanks to the disgust plastered on Eclipse's face. It was the little things in life that kept me amused.

"Sorry about leaving you on the roof. Looks like you don't need rescuing." He pauses before eyeing Eclipse. His face remained neutral as he stared down at the leader of the Guild. "Or do you?"

Eclipse took his drink off the counter and put down the exact change. "We can finish our chat later." Chat? I assumed that was a two-way street instead of being on the receiving end of a monologue. But I gave him a nod before I returned to EO.

"Midnight Alley custom." I grab a bottle of tequila off

the top shelf. Filling two shot glasses, I put a lime next to each. "A shot on the house for saving one of the staff."

He laughed. "In Vanguard? You'll go broke with a policy like that. I'm sure half your wait staff got kidnapped by lunch." He grabbed the glass and held it up in a toast. "May all the men I save be as sexy as you." We clicked glasses before slamming the drinks.

He wasn't coy. My cheeks turned red. Thankfully, I could blame the alcohol. I admired his forearms and the dusting of hair disguising the muscles. I always wondered if they were strong before heroes acquired their powers or if it was a byproduct of their origin story.

"Thanks for the rescue earlier. I should have known better."

"Don't go into alleys," we said in unison.

"Yup, I remember that lecture in class. And what's with villains hiding in alleys, anyway? Do they think it's adding to their mystique?" EO asked the important questions.

"Right? Who wants to smell like trash?"

I held up the bottle of tequila, ready to pour another shot. "I don't need to be drunk for you to take advantage of me. But I'll take a beer though, dark, preferably Belgian."

No words. I stammered as I set the bottle down. He could tear open holes in reality, but Bernard would declare his *actual* power was silencing me. I might not be speaking, but I was aware of the tightness in my pants. Thankfully, the bar hid the growing erection, though part of me wished it didn't.

"Who is that asshat?"

"Eclipse? Poseur. He wants all the status with none of the work. The HeroApp™ says he's done zero heroic deeds. Instead, he comes here trying to climb the social ladder. You're much better company."

"And here I am, covered in snake venom."

"Speaking of,"—I pulled a beer from the cooler, popping the cap on the side of the counter—"I haven't seen you in here before."

"I've been here about a month. My alter ego got transferred from Guardian City for work. Every city needs saving, but a paycheck is important. With any luck, one of the superhero teams is looking for an addition."

I handed him his beer, watching closely as he took a sip. I wanted to see his face without the mask. It covered his eyes, and I wanted to see if they sparkled as much as his personality.

"You'll never be bored here. We're about due for an alien invasion. Centurions handle the big threats, but they play well with others. We have a pretty healthy amount of street vigilantes, but you can barely walk a block without—
"

"Being lured into a dark alley and attacked by a snake woman?" He laughed. "Vanguard isn't boring." He gave me a once over. "And it's getting more interesting by the minute."

EO was a player. I had seen the type. Hell, I *was* that type. There was no point in being coy when you found somebody who got a rise out of your lil' sidekick. I was about to ask him about his plans for later when I caught the shimmer of a wedding band on his finger. I wasn't one to judge, but I had a rule about married men. They came with baggage. When they could hurl cars, I avoided drama at all costs.

"Married?"

"Happily," he said. "He should be here shortly."

"Hero?"

"Yeah, but we don't partner together most of the time. We want to make our own names in the industry."

"How noble of you."

"Jealous?" he asked. There was a particular type of married man, the one comfortable with the ring around his finger and the protections it offered. They talked a big game, but at the end of the night, you knew who they were going home with. I had been a guest star in more than one relationship, but more often than not, it got awkward.

"Not even a little," I lied. I grabbed another bottle of beer, popped the cap, and set it down next to him. "Don't forget to tip your bartender," I added with a smile.

"Just the tip?"

Touché. He knew how to get my engine running. It was

going to be a long night of teasing, but this hero had met his match. If we were going to play this game, it was him that'd need rescuing.

He pulled out his phone. With a quick scan of a text, he opened a portal to his side. It took a second before an overly muscular hero emerged. Okay, there had to be something in the water in Guardian City to produce these two studs. Maybe they fell into the same vat of dangerous chemicals? Either way, I could see I was going to have myself a fun night of flirting.

"Stonewall," he gestured to his partner, "meet…"

"Alejandro." I handed him a beer. "EO has been telling me all about you."

The edge of his lip turned up. "So you're the sexy bear he rescued."

My face went from warm to hot. Had I met my match?

A couple months ago, all but one superhero had been depowered. How? I don't know. It had something to do with a demon. But since then, heroes had been cagey about going out. Tonight, however, Midnight Alley didn't have an empty table, and the staff moved with a purpose. It wasn't standing room only, but we were getting close.

While I mixed my millionth "Cape Chaser" cocktail, I split the shaker in two, pouring one, two, three drinks into chilled martini glasses. The Furies, a trio of magical heroes, applauded as I pushed drinks across the bar.

"Alejandro." Alecto bent over, sipping without lifting the glass. "We fought Hades tonight, and yet, you're the hero." The other two followed suit, eyes wide as they savored my handiwork. I lived for the admiration. While they saved the city, I did my best to reward them for doing what I couldn't.

"Maybe if Hades had a few drinks in him, he wouldn't be such an uptight blowhard." I shot the ladies a wink.

They giggled, leaving money on the counter and heading toward the music. Like always, the Furies wanted to be as close to the DJ as possible. With a quick wipe of the rag, I was ready for the next patron to order a drink.

By the entrance, Bruno guarded the door, keeping out the riffraff. I gave him a chin nod when he pointed to his eyes with two fingers. He then pointed across the club. The frantic motion meant urgent, and I followed until I caught the source of his panic. Eclipse and Scarlet were seated in a booth, talking.

We had seen Scarlet stare down the biggest power-houses in the industry. Even as a petite woman, she had the fortitude of a titan. If she didn't want to speak with Eclipse, she'd have pivoted away with grace. When grace didn't work, she'd *make* him go away. She had a serious face as the two of them talked. Nothing good would come of it.

I eyed Bruno again, trying to shove all the confusion

into raised eyebrows and a disgusted frown. Bruno shook his head before doing the finger thing again. This time he gestured wildly, almost pointing at me. I put a hand on my chest, trying to make sense of his inefficient communication system.

"Alejandro, how's it going?"

Oh, Bruno meant for me to turn around. We needed to work on his hand signals. I didn't need to see him to know the voice. Lars, no real superhero name. It was hard to pick a single reason why I didn't call him after our first encounter. There were many. So damned many.

"Lars," I feigned a smile. "What can I get you?"

As I turned, he leaned on the bar in his signature blue spandex suit with a plunging neckline that almost reached his navel. His chest was just as hairy as I remembered it, and I fondly remember running my hands through it. But that's where the evening took a turn for weird.

"Whatever." He gestured toward the beer taps. "I just came over to see you."

The Men of Vanguard were some of the sexiest men on Earth. I had a PhD in male studies, so we should consider my opinion expert testimony. But they were also some of the most out of sorts. Lars had made it clear he was into me a few nights ago. He seemed like a fun guy, always down for a laugh, and shapeshifters were pretty thrilling in bed. Lars was anything but thrilling.

"I was hoping for a second date, maybe dinner?"

As Chad would say, "Let's run down the list of no." Lars and I never had a date. We had lackluster sex. I'm clear about my expectations. There's no point in leading a guy on. Despite that, once the deed was done, he wanted to spend the night in bed cuddling. I convinced him it would not happen. He already irked me that he had over-promised and under-delivered. I knew for the next time that I had to inquire what type of shapeshifter. Being able to turn yourself into inanimate objects... Yeah, not the night of mind-blowing sex I hoped for.

"I'm not sure that's a good idea."

As I filled a pint glass with our cheapest beer, he scooted closer to whisper. "You were the best sex I've ever had." Of course I was. Just because he was phoning it in didn't mean I had to. I maintained my high standards.

"It's obvious you want something more. The last thing I need in my life is a relationship." Clear. Concise. I'd pat myself on the back for the honesty.

"You won't know if you don't try, right?"

I don't respond well to pressure. More than that, I hated when a man attempted to convince me they knew what I needed. I set the beer on the counter, my face void of emotion.

"No."

"If you just let me..."

"Alejandro, did you still want to come to my place after you, uh, get off." EO, my hero. I would have said yes to just about any offer. I prayed for a villain to blow up the club to end this conversation.

"Yeah, but I won't be the only one getting off." EO set his drink on the bar and gave me a wink. That was the third time tonight he had rescued me. The snake woman remained the least infuriating encounter.

"Oh," Lars said, taking his beer. "I guess you're just another tease." He turned around and walked off, not giving me a second thought.

"Shape-shifting? I think distorting reality is his real superpower."

"Some guys don't know how to take no for an answer."

All night, EO and his husband had laughed together. Every now and then, they'd hold up an empty bottle, and I'd do my job and make sure another beer waited for them. There had been flirting and more than one innuendo. Some guys just know how to make conversation effortless. More than once, Stonewall called me out for eyeing his man. It would have been embarrassing, except EO would make a quick comment by taking the heat off me.

This is how threesomes started. Which could have been fun, but I tried to remember how often they went sideways. While Stonewall was a rock solid stud of a man, he wasn't my type. EO, on the other hand, I wanted to drag my tongue across what I hoped was a hairy chest.

"What happened to Stonewall?"

"He's somewhere in the Middle East, stopping a drug lord from destroying a city."

"Oh," I laughed, "sounds mundane when you say it like that."

"So..." He leaned over the bar. I waited for him to finish the statement, but he almost seemed nervous. Just because they wear a mask and stop bad guys doesn't mean they have nerves of steel. Saving the world, easy, but having an intimate conversation, decimated the strongest amongst them.

I cleared the empty glasses off the bar top and picked up the tips lying on the damp surface. Tonight would end with a pretty healthy wad of cash in my pocket. Things were good until I remembered that my employment had an expiration date. Scarlet, damn you.

"Would you like to go out?"

"You mean to your place?" Okay, maybe I cut through the formalities a bit too quickly.

"I was thinking, more like a date?"

"Oh." This was a first. Half the heroes in here had open relationships, letting them bed who they wanted. But never had one of them asked me on a date. I made it a rule to not indulge men who cheated on their partners.

"What would Stonewall say?"

He handed me a napkin. The logo for the Alley had been folded in half. I raised an eyebrow, ready to crumple it before throwing it away.

"Read it, you goof."

Opening the triangle, I could barely read the scribbles. "He thinks your cote. You have my blessing. Cote? Is that a new slang word the kids are using?"

EO slapped his forehead. "Cute. I think you're cute."

I eyed the napkin again. Had his husband just given him permission to go on a date? I had encountered a lot of arrangements, but nothing quite like this. I didn't quite know what to say. Did I want to see EO out of his uniform? That was a Texas-sized 10-4. But dealing with the fallout of a complicated hookup, didn't exactly make my penis hard.

"Think about it. In the meantime, here's my number." He handed me a second napkin. I was about to refuse, to avoid the complications, when I caught the smile stretched across his face. Damn, he was charming and sexy. I rescinded my earlier comment. Penis approached full mast.

"I will." I wanted to pull that suit off and ride him until I ached. Some people have a little devil on their shoulder convincing them to do bad things. Mine resided in my pants.

"Good." The portal opened, and he stepped backward. With a quick waggle of the eyebrow, the stud vanished to who knows where.

"You're playing with fire, Al," I mumbled.

5

"W E HAVE LIVE COVERAGE OF THE FACTORY BEING DESTROYED BY *the Nocturnals. Megan, what do we know?"*

I rarely watched the news, but the breaking update interjected itself on every channel. The city in peril provided white noise as I scrubbed down the bar and reset after a busy night. Tonight's tips were well earned, but it also meant that my station was a mess.

"We've been told there are five members of this frightful team. As of now, we've only seen three. But they are demolishing the factory. Explosions continue to go off in the wings of the building. We do not know why they would attack this location. At the moment, we have no idea what it contains."

One of the bar backs dropped a box of bottles on the counter as I watched the footage from the helicopter. "For your empties." I turned around to examine the rows of alcohol to see there were a good number of near-empty bottles.

"Gracias, Shawn. Can you grab the trash? Otherwise, I think I'm good."

"No hay problema."

"*Oh, no!*" the woman on the television screamed. I glanced up just in time to see a large piece of equipment from the factory flying toward the reporter. There was shouting before the screen turned to static. Ever since the depowering, villains found a new sense of zeal in their schemes. Before, it had almost been comical. Now they doubled down in their efforts, and it seemed as if the heroes were being run ragged.

The screen cut to a man in the studio. "*We're getting word that Megan is safe. The news chopper is making an emergency landing. We have yet to find any information behind the attack, but we'll keep you posted.*"

"It's getting bad out there," Bruno said. I placed a bottle of tequila on the shelf. "I wouldn't want to be a hero right now."

Bruno's comment supported my earlier thought. The heroes of Vanguard City didn't seem to be winning this war. "What do you think they want this time?" I asked.

"That's part of what's changed. Before, it was like they always had an agenda. Revenge. Money. Fame. Alien technology to make themselves overlord of humanity. Now? They just destroy things and terrorize without rhyme or reason." I didn't realize that Bruno spent time studying the motives of villains.

Bruno handed me bottles from the box until I finished replacing the empties. The reporter continued speaking, but didn't add new information. "What changed?" I asked.

"Heroes across the globe lost their powers. They were powerless. That kind of fear would give me performance anxiety," he said.

I had to agree. "Did you see that guy from the Guild tonight, Eclipse? Powered people like that," I growled, "they should be out there doing some good. But instead, they're basking in their own glory. Hopefully, more good guys stand up and protect the city."

"Speaking of heroes..." Bruno didn't hide his knowing grin. He was about to give me grief about my newest fans. "Come out with it, Al."

"Out with what?" I preferred playing coy. I didn't like to plaster my escapades across the wall, especially not with the staff. Of course, they knew my reputation. It came up frequently in conversation, but I didn't need to feed into—

"Are you going to peg him?"

Blunt. "I don't know." It was the truth. "I think he asked me out on a date? But I'm not so sure."

"Have a nice dinner. Drink a few drinks. End the night with your skivvies around your ankles. What isn't there to like about this?"

"He has a husband," I blurted. Okay, coy wasn't exactly

my best trait. I held out for almost a minute. That might be a record.

"Cheater?"

I shook my head. "I don't think so. His husband gave his blessing."

"Is it just sex? Or like a proper date?"

I eyed Bruno. For a burly bouncer who could easily bench press me with one hand, he had a soft streak. That grizzly exterior only made the squishy bits more charming. Once you got to know him, the scary persona he exuded while working the door melted away. If only our handsome bouncer played for my team.

"An actual date? I think. Maybe. I'm not sure."

"Oh. Sounds like they're polyamorous. Could be a good situation for you."

Poly-ama-what? Bruno dropped the information like every human being on the planet knew the definition. I cycled through my education as a gay man, and nowhere had that term popped up. My raised eyebrow or lack of quip made him laugh.

"It means they're open to dating more than each other. Think of it like an open relationship with feelings."

My experiences with open relationships had been questionable in the past. It should be the ideal situation, sex, and then they head home. But the idea of dating a man who would go home to his partner? That seemed almost greedy.

"Wait—" I threw the towel over my shoulder. "So they are married, but they date other people? Doesn't that screw over the new guy? What if things got serious?"

"Alejandro, I wouldn't have taken you for such a traditional definition of marriage. Who says you can't have two partners? Back in college, I dated a couple for a while. Luca and Brianne. It was pretty awesome. We got along great, and always felt like there was somebody around when I needed them."

"Luca? Bruno, did you just admit to having a gay relationship?"

He laughed. "Are you calling me a prude? Luca and I never really played alone. But I didn't mind having another guy in bed with Brianne there."

"What if I had no interest in his husband?"

"Did the husband ask you out on a date?"

"Well..." I tried to think if the husband had given me any signals that he was interested. "I guess not."

"Get out of your head. Call the guy and enjoy a date. It's not like you're moving in."

It all seemed very complicated, and that was before making the phone call. I didn't like dealing with complications. I was probably the least complicated guy with sex, but this? Sharing a guy? I didn't know about that. That threw up a thousand red flags and at the end of the experience, I'd be heartbroken and alone.

"Maybe..." It was a lie, but I didn't want Bruno to know that.

"I should give Brianne a call and see what they're up to these days."

I shook my head. "A Bruno sandwich." I laughed. "That's not a bad image." I gave the man a wink and returned to cleaning down the beer taps. I didn't have to worry about calling EO tonight. Despite the hero's willingness to save me from being snake food, I wasn't convinced I needed that kind of complication in my life.

<hr>

"This isn't the right way."

"The road is washed out," the cab driver responded.

"You can take the overpass."

"This way is faster," he said.

I hated when people told me how to pour drinks, so I sat back and let the taxi driver do his job. I was certain I was right, but he would not have it. If it hadn't been pouring, I'd have told him to pull over, and I'd walk home. I hated being wet, and the moment it reached my socks I'd be miserable.

My phone vibrated.

Sir Awesome: You free tonight? Have something *awesome* to show you.

It vibrated again before I could reply.

Dark Star: Want to come by the Lunar Base?

My phone hadn't stopped buzzing for the last half hour. The heroes of Vanguard prepared to hang their capes up for the night. Once off the job, they were eagerly hoping I'd help them slide out of their spandex tights and slide into, well, me. But as much as I wanted some uncomplicated fun, I couldn't help but keep thinking about what Bruno said.

"You're literally going to the wrong side of the city."

"Do you want to drive?" My backseat navigating didn't thrill the cabbie. I wanted to reach through the break in the plastic and strangle him with his scarf. I had been spending too much time with Xander.

"Just stop," I said, "I'll walk."

If I had said that fifteen minutes ago, it wouldn't have been a big deal. At this point, it would take me at least an hour to get myself home. I didn't have time to dwell on the impending moistness. The driver slammed the breaks, skidding to a stop. He popped the locks on the door.

"Do I tell you how to do your job?" He turned, sneering. "Get out."

I had barely gotten out and shut the door before he dropped the gas and peeled away. I ran across the sidewalk under an old movie theater sign. It had been years since they had shown a movie. By the way the boarded-up doors struggled to stay on their hinges, I imagined vandals claimed the building for themselves.

I examined the map on my phone. I had been right. The driver had taken me to the outskirts of Southland. This part of the city was dangerous enough during the day that taxis avoided it. Getting one at this hour was going to be impossible. When I scanned the available car services, they weren't much better.

"Well, tonight is going to suck."

The phone vibrated. A dozen missed texts.

Astroman: I want you to fuck me again.

"I'm not making that mistake again." My finger hovered over the message, prepared to delete it when I remembered he could fly. "I mean, putting out would keep me dry." I should have slapped myself. "Have standards, Al."

Lightning tore through the sky, followed by a grumble of thunder that shook the city. If I had considered walking, the renewed vigor of the falling rain had me reconsidering. I wouldn't make it to the end of the block before I turned into a squishy mess. Mother Nature forced my hand.

I pulled a folded napkin from my pocket. Punching in the number, I took a steadying breath. "Here goes nothing." I sent the message. It was a long shot. EO could be off saving the world or be curled in bed playing little spoon to Stonewall. I didn't have high—

"You didn't have to concoct an emergency to get my attention. A simple 'how's it going, you handsome stud' would have been enough."

The amusement in his tone made me smile. I turned

around to see my bearded savior. I tried to play it noncha-lant, but the sight of EO put sinister ideas in my head. And my pants. "I had been trying to get kidnapped, but nobody took the bait tonight."

"A win for me then."

"What is that? Three times you've come to my rescue tonight?"

"Four technically, but who's counting?"

I wish I could see his face without the mask. Most superheroes thought it made them look more striking, but I found it hid their best quality. I liked a muscular man covered in soft padding, but it was always the eyes that caught my attention. EO's mask left space for his nose and beard, but the part covering his eyes left them white voids. Unfortunately, never being sure who was under the mask was par for the course when dealing with caped crusaders.

"Are you up to anything? I mean, do you have any plans? I-I-"

"EO, are you asking me to hang out?" Dammit, he was even more charming as he tripped over his words. The cocky persona fell away, and I saw a nervous man stepping into his shoes. Despite texting him for another dutiful save, he reverted into an awkward teenage boy.

"A handsome man like you? I wasn't sure if your dance card was full."

"Funny," I said. "I was thinking the same thing."

Two portals opened, one to his left, the other to his

right. I recognized the front door to the club in the one to his left. It wasn't exactly close to my house, but anything would be better than Southland. The other portal, however, was nearly blinding as light poured out, cutting through the dreary night.

"I like options." He knew how to slip in a double entendre. My phone had a dozen unanswered text messages of men looking to have their clothes torn off. But this stud, he maintained just enough mystery to keep me on the hook. This was a lesson to all the desperate men out there, play it cool. I might let little Alejandro do the driving most of the time, but even he enjoyed being wooed.

Taking a step toward the portal filled with light, I paused, unsure of what I was about to get myself into. "I'm not about to fall into a forest fire? It doesn't lead to the sun?"

The other portal closed, and he wrapped a hand around my waist as he guided me into the light. For the second time that night, EO held me close. I hated to admit it, but I didn't mind being rescued by this hero. It almost felt, dare I say it... Right?

What had I gotten myself into?

6

"I DON'T HAVE WORDS."

This never happened. I had a quip for every situation. But as the sun broke the horizon and light poured across the white buildings of Paris, I lacked the vocabulary to capture the beauty. I imagined this was one of those moments that would move Griffin to tears, and I understood why.

"I hoped this would make up for being ditched in the rain."

Atop the Eiffel Tower, the city of Paris sprawled out in every direction. I thought Vanguard had congested areas, but Paris seemed to be nothing more than narrow streets weaving around a plethora of buildings older than the United States. As the seconds sped by, sunlight found its way down each street, breathing life into the city.

"Consider your debt paid."

EO leaned on the railing, stealing a glance at the hundreds of feet below. From this vantage point, it was difficult to understand just how high we were. There were few people walking about the tower, all appearing no larger than ants. Even the noise of a waking city couldn't penetrate the roar of the breeze. It was the next best thing to flying through the clouds.

Griffin and Xander would tease me for chasing capes. But how often did their dates bring them to such a wonderous landmark? I'd overlook the fact we were trespassing on a national monument. There was a good chance that in the last week, EO had somehow been involved in saving the thing from a mad Frenchman. Villains loved destroying monuments. It was basically 'Evil Doer 101.'

"Thank you." I was prepared to crawl into bed, cranky and cursing the world. Between Scarlet selling the club and a taxi drive from hell, this had not been my night.

"I kind of owed you after leaving you on the rooftop. Not my best hero-ing moment." He leaned against me, nudging me with his shoulder. Some would say getting naked was the most intimate act between two people. Obviously, they never stood shoulder-to-shoulder with a handsome man while watching the sun rise over Paris.

"Why here?"

"Would you prefer the Australian Outback? With a

little effort, I bet I could find the International Space Station or the colony on the moon."

I laughed. "No, this is perfect." He put his hand on the middle of my back. Delivering flowers would have been laying it on thick, but the sunrise? He was on a mission to impress.

"It's quiet," he confessed. "There are a million people waking up, living their lives. But up here, it's quiet. You don't get to experience that much anymore."

Midnight Alley was home, and I loved the fast-paced life of being a bartender. In a night, I can have a thousand interactions with the patrons. By the end, I was charged and ready to take on the world. If I could make the perfect Margarita, there was nothing I couldn't achieve.

"I like the noise," I admitted. "Not the constant horns or screaming, but the city is alive. There's rarely a moment you can breathe. I don't know. I've always been surrounded by people. This..." I gestured to the entirety of Paris. "This borders on eerie. Es hermoso, but still eerie."

For a moment, I feared my honesty had spoiled a moment. But I caught him nodding. "I need it every once in a while. After this, I'm charged and ready to go." He cracked his neck before rolling his shoulders. "A little R&R, and then I can go back to saving the world."

"Speaking of," I laughed, "what is your origin story? Chemicals? Messenger from God?"

"You're going to laugh."

"I know a guy bit by a radioactive cockroach. Trust me, there is nothing sexy about scurrying away when somebody turns on the lights."

"A few years ago, I was working as a temp at a science lab. My only job was to put files in alphabetical order. Man, I hated that job. There were all these people with lab coats way too smart for their own good. I graduated with a degree in communications, and I still couldn't figure out what they were talking about."

"Explosion in the lab?"

"Less explosion," he laughed. "More like I walked into a secure room just as they were attempting to manipulate dark matter. Apparently, the giant sign reading, 'Do Not Enter' wasn't big enough. They considered the experiment a failure. If only they knew it changed my body and gave me the ability to tear holes in space and time."

"In case you do interviews, bend the truth." I patted him on the chest. The glass of his vest had turned chilly, and I imagined he must be freezing. "Tell them someone trapped a child in there and you rescued them from death. Everybody loves a little selfless tragedy."

"You've got experience with this?" When his eyebrow lifted, he turned from stoic to... well, Paris was the second most beautiful thing I had seen today. I wanted to slide my hand up his chest, along his neck, and feel the softness of his beard. Then I'd need to feel it against my face, for verification, of course.

"One of my friends works for the Beacon and always talks about superheroes. The other works public relations for the Centurions." I neglected to mention Bernard was also Sentinel. Had EO ever partnered with them? I'd think his ability to transport across the globe would be an asset to a premiere superhero team.

"Oh, and here I thought it all came from your experience with supers in the club." He gave me a smirk and an exaggerated wink. "And out of the club."

The mention of my recreational hobbies threw a wrench into the plans. If he was only interested in getting his rocks off, why bring me here? EO might not be as one-dimensional as the heroes I was used to bringing home. I was about to ask about his intentions when he held a finger up to my lips.

"My turn. What's your origin story?"

Nobody had ever asked. I was known as the fun one, the talker, and I had a knack for always moving the conversation forward. I'm sure Bernard would say I used it as a defense mechanism, but EO had cut me off before I spit out a pithy joke.

"No explosions. Mi madre moved to Vanguard from Mexico City when I was a little boy. Salvación hadn't declared himself the protector of the city back then. It was dangerous to be on the streets. We moved in with my uncle and his family. I remember little about Mexico. But the city had life to it. That's probably why I like people so much."

I kept my uncle's death at the hands of the Duo of Disaster to myself. The heroes didn't make it to him in time. It nearly broke my family, and still to this day, mi madre referred to him as if he might walk through the door. It was one reason why I loved my job. Surrounded by heroes, even the worst of them, there was a sense of safety. Like today, there was always a brave super ready to swoop in and save the day.

"Why did you ask me out?"

"When snake woman attacked, you hardly flinched."

"You know how often women have—"

"Serious." Damn, EO played for keeps.

"Being normal, especially in Vanguard, you either live in fear or go with the flow."

"You stared down a villain. Then you stared down Eclipse."

"He's an ass."

"And yet, you got uncomfortable when that guy asked for a second date. You're either a master actor, or you're brave when you need to be, but you still care about people. Consider me intrigued."

"And I thought it's because I'm—"

"Hot? Yeah, that doesn't hurt." If I didn't know better, I'd say he could read minds or perhaps predict the future. I'd have to research black matter when I got home. I'm sure Wikipedia could answer, "Does exposure to black matter give me the ability to read minds?"

"What about your husband?"

"Ju—Stonewall," he corrected the slip of the tongue quickly. "He's the one who encouraged me to ask."

"But—"

"This is new for you?"

I answered by turning into the sunlight. It had risen enough that it was nearly impossible to see the city through the searing light. I had more questions than I could sort through. Most of them I feared would make me look foolish or naïve. I might have a PhD in the bedroom, but I remained willfully ignorant to any relationship that wasn't part of prime-time sitcoms.

"I'd like to answer what I can."

Like a guardian angel, I could hear Bernard's voice whispering over my shoulder. He'd tell me to live in the moment and meter out my insecurities instead of letting them ruin a majestic moment. Papi had a point. This sexy man had saved me multiple times in a single night, and I was putting fear in front of what could be a wonderful moment.

"Later. If you don't mind."

I stepped closer to him, our arms touching. I leaned my head on his shoulder. The sharp edges of his costume made it less than comfortable, but as he slid his arm around my waist, giving me a squeeze, it didn't matter. Alone on the Eiffel Tower made this dangerously close to the ending scene of a Hallmark movie. When he leaned his head against mine, my chest tightened. Roll the end credits; we had reached a perfect conclusion to the night.

It lasted for minutes until I feared the orbs in my vision would become permanent. Time was running out for our moment. Eventually, one of us would comment on needing to return to Vanguard City, and this would become another memory. I wouldn't forget it anytime soon, but—

He broke the silence. "We should—"

"Not yet."

I spun about, the sun to my back, unable to make out his face while my eyesight adjusted. I held my hand against his cheek, the softness of his beard against my palm. My thumb touched the edge of his lips, providing a destination. As I leaned in, I swore he smelled of sandalwood and leather. He cupped my face as he met me halfway, our lips barely grazing one another.

I leaned forward, expecting to find a taste that matched the scent of his beard. EO pulled back, just far enough to avoid a first kiss. I would have retreated except for the tightening of the skin at the edge of his mouth, a grin if I ever felt one. I lingered like a school child waiting for their first kiss behind the bleachers.

EO tasted like cinnamon.

His lips pressed against mine, his mustache tickling the underside of my nose. When he parted his lips, he slowed, holding my bottom lip between his teeth. He didn't move as he held me in place. The entirety of Europe mirrored me as

I held my breath, savoring the sensation of this beautiful man seizing control of the moment.

We broke apart. I could tell by his expression, that this outing had reached its end. Was I being selfish as I considered asking him to stay for another hour, maybe two? The kiss had been wonderful, but there was a list of things I wanted to do to him, *with* him. I wanted to check as many boxes before...

Before? What? He left? Returned home to Stonewall? My brain picked at the moment until it found the insecurity. Just like that, standing on the Eiffel Tower, watching the sunrise with a handsome man, didn't seem to outweigh the reality.

"Penny for your thoughts?"

I forced a weak smile. "Nothing, just in my head. I had a good time."

"Me too, handsome. I hope it's not the only sunrise we see."

The portal opened and just beyond, I could see the front door of Midnight Alley. He gave my hand a squeeze as I walked through.

"Call me." I turned around, and the portal had vanished. Just like that, an amazing morning vanished, and I was left in the darkness of Vanguard.

7

———

X: WAKE UP. BREAKFAST WAITS FOR NO MAN.

G: Huzzah.

X: Al, don't make me deal with him alone.

G: I hope you get decaf.

B: Adding Huzzah to the banned word list.

X: Ha!

G: Al, wipe off the lube and hurry.

A: I hate you all.

B: Huzzah.

G: Wtf?

B: Yeah, it felt wrong. Banned.

The black-out curtains struggled to keep the sun from intruding on my bedroom. The downside to working at a bar was sleeping half the day. Thankfully, I didn't require more than a few hours. The light hit the full-length mirror at the foot of the bed and got dangerously close to reflecting it in my eyes. It was the price I paid for being able to get a better view while on all fours.

I eyed my phone from under the covers as the conversation continued to scroll by. They'd be insufferable until I agreed to go. When had I missed breakfast with them? Out of the four, I was the most consistent. Sleep had been elusive. Instead, I spent the last few hours tossing and turning, thinking about EO leaving me and returning home to Stonewall.

Was I jealous? I didn't get jealous. Did I? But as I thought of him jumping through a portal and climbing into bed with Stonewall, something tightened in my chest. "Dammit, that's definitely jealousy."

A: Fine, I'm on my way.
X: Huzzah!
G: Ass.

With a flick of the finger, the HeroApp™ appeared on the screen. The first photo that appeared was EO wrestling with the snake woman. The muscles under his suit rippled as he used a portal to slam a dumpster into the villain. It was impressive to see how he used his abilities. He might be sexy, but there was plenty of skill inside that... inside that suit. I had to admit, I was sad he hadn't followed me through the portal so I could escort him to my apartment.

Looking past the phone, I could see the bulge in the covers. It seemed I wasn't the only one disappointed I hadn't peeled him out of his armor. With a slight squeeze through the blanket, I moaned. Yeah, I needed to take care of this or I'd jump somebody at the HideOut.

Minutes later, I was standing in the spray from the shower. While the rest of the apartment was nothing to write home about, the shower took up an entire end of the bathroom with large stone tile. It served as my secret base, the place where I hid from the rest of the world while I prepared to save the day. Okay, maybe that was a bit of an overshot, but as the spray pulsed between my shoulder blades, I didn't care about anything else.

Almost anything.

I'd have gladly escorted EO into my lair. I imagined that barrel chest pressed against my back. His muscular arms wrapped around my chest, dragging the soap along my chest. There'd be a flick of my nipple and I'd moan. It'd be sweet... until it wasn't. No matter how innocent, him naked would have me rock hard. Even now, my cock bounced up and down at the idea of him grinding against the cheeks of my ass.

Between the water pelting my skin and the cool air of

the bathroom, I was in heaven. The guys can wait. It wouldn't be the first time they had to order a second coffee while I hunted for my underwear at somebody's house. This might not be as epic a tale, but my cock didn't care.

I played coy as I ran the soap over my neck, lathering until it coated my stubble. While I might not sport a full-grown beard, my chest hair made up for it. As I looked down at the dark hair, the water pushed it down, almost forming an arrow to my cock. There was no point in ignoring it, not that it'd let me.

Running my palm along the underside of my cock, my skin turned prickly, and I let out a sigh with the shudder. Most of the time, soap and a little imagination were all I'd need to shake a pestering erection. This wasn't most of the time. This morning needed a little extra something to get my day started.

Half stepping out of the shower, I reached into the vanity drawer and pulled out my favorite inanimate shower buddy, complete with suction cup. The lifelike dildo was thick enough to leave me feeling it for the rest of the day. For today's roleplaying scenario, I'd be imagining it belonged to a teleporting superhero who needed to blow his load.

With a little spit and a firm grip, I pressed it against the wall. The suction cup sealed, and my make-believe-man-friend was ready to slide across the sweet spot inside my ass. Closing my eyes, I dragged my fingers down the length of the shaft and imagined EO smiling at me as he stared down at me. He wouldn't need to say a word, just a glance at his cock and I'd gladly service the stud.

My cock twitched with approval.

With my back to EO, I'd start with the teasing, nestling his cock against my ass. Much like my chest, my ass was covered in a dusting of dark hair. His cock would shine as I pushed backward, making sure he was nice and hard.

Spitting into my hand, I reached back, coating the head of the toy, hoping this would be the moment he'd slide his hands up my back, gripping my shoulders. I wanted him to push, bending me over with a primal need to bury his cock. I gripped my shaft and gave it a few quick strokes, sliding the foreskin over the head. The toy pressed against the entrance to my ass and I had to stop. Imagining EO using me to unload apparently was the inspiration I needed to make this a quick shower.

"EO," I whispered.

I leaned back, relishing the sensation as it stretched me open. I wanted to tease his head, to pull away as he tried to bury his cock, but his hands on my shoulders wouldn't give me the option. Sliding further down the shaft, I let out a gasp. I eagerly wanted to reach the base and feel his balls slap against my cheeks. It was almost too much, and I had to count my breaths to keep from exploding across the tiled floor.

Holding still, I flexed my muscles, hoping he was vocal,

loud enough to know that he appreciated me giving up my ass. With a little wiggle, I reached the base. No matter how realistic a fake cock promised, the testicles never delivered a lifelike experience. Nothing felt as amazing when a top sawed in and out, their balls smacking against the perineum.

"Come in me." It bordered on begging, and given the chance, I'd gladly do the same in person. The idea of EO holding my hips, burying his cock in me as he unloaded had my balls tightening against my body.

Standing up, the toy pressed against my prostate. I slowed my hand, letting the foreskin gather over my cock. I rocked back and forth, and the orgasm shot through my body like an electric shock. Biting my lower lip, I watched as the cum shot in ropes across the shower.

It had only been forty-eight hours since I last came, but by the flood of cum leaking from my cock, you'd think I had been chaste for a year. As the ripples of pleasure faded, now came the hard part. While my cock deflated, I still had a fairly large object wedged inside my body.

"I swear," I gasped as I slid forward. "How is it I can take that while hard..."

"... but the moment you come, it's like you made poor life choices."

Chad set a plate with a bagel sandwich in front of me while he handed Xander a plate of sausages. No eggs, no toast, just sausage. I would have to file that away in the weird habits folder. I loved the man, but as he tore into the first link, I nearly commented.

Chad returned with a tray and four more coffees for the table. I'd keep ordering until he threatened to cut me off. "What about when he has you folded in half? Legs on his shoulder and you're feeling like a million bucks. Then you come and..."

"It's like you forgot you had a bad hip," Bernard finished for him.

Griffin snorted. "Except in your case—"

Bernard pointed across the table at Griffin, his arm threatening to detach and smack the man. "Finish that sentence, and I *will* end you."

Xander bumped fists with Griffin. The morning had barely begun and already the well-oiled machine known as the breakfast club was in full swing. For all the things going on inside my head, this, these people, they made all my worries melt away. Bernard's face turning bright red didn't hurt either.

These were the best friends a guy could ask for. They were the type of guys who dropped everything to support a friend in need. We all had our quirks, but instead of focusing on our differences, we met regularly at the HideOut to talk about the things that brought us together.

You couldn't beat the smell of freshly brewed coffee, baked goods, and conversations involving penises.

"Are we skipping small talk today? Are we getting right into where Alejandro got prodded this morning?"

I stuck my tongue out at Griffin. "I think somebody isn't getting prodded enough with that kind of statement. Do I need to have a chat with Sebastian?"

"Once he moves in, you'll be getting prodded a couple times a day." Xander gave Griffin a wink. "Or are you the one prodding?"

Griffin rolled his eyes back in his head. "I take it all back. Alejandro, tell us a tale. Psychics? Birdmen? What about that pirate from the future?"

Captain Yar, that man knew how to plunder—

"Nope. I'm hijacking the conversation," Bernard said. Normally, he didn't get involved until he finished half his coffee. He had more pep in his step than usual. Was Bernard getting prodded? I wonder if he'd let me watch that show?

"The floor is yours," I said.

"Oh no, it's still about you." His eyes narrowed as he leaned forward. I admired the man's perfectly manicured beard. It smelled of lavender, and the fact I could tell he washed with beard conditioner meant he was getting dangerously close.

"What did I do?"

"Anything you want to tell us about yesterday?"

"Nothing special." I'd lie until I couldn't. I know, I know, usually I was willing to throw out the most graphic details of my life. But I hadn't quite wrapped my head around the situation with EO.

"Griffin."

Griffin pulled out his phone. With a couple flicks of the finger. He dropped it in front of me. A pedestrian had snapped a photo of me in the alley and EO rescuing me from the snake lady. All three sets of eyes stared at me, urging me to come clean.

"I almost got eaten before work. Nothing new there. Griffin, weren't you held hostage in a bank last Monday?"

"Xander, is Alejandro being dodgy?"

"Very. He's hiding something." Great, all three of them were in on it. Against one of them, I might stand a chance. But Bernard had a sixth sense, and with the other two in his corner, it was only a matter of time before they ferreted out the details of what happened after.

"What about work?"

I don't know what they were fishing for, but Bernard would not let this go. Usually, I wasn't the one in the hot seat. I suddenly had sympathy for Griffin when we grilled him about his love life.

"Scarlet is selling Midnight Alley. I'm trying not to think about it. I love my job. Hell, I love the club. She mentioned selling it to an employee. But damn, we work at a club and none of us have that kind of money."

"I say this with love." Whenever Xander started a sentence that way, it was about to be a kick to the ego. "But I can't see you as an owner. The stress would be rough."

I nearly jumped as Chad rested a hand on my shoulder. The man's superhuman ability to waltz in and out of a dozen conversations bordered on eerie. He gave my shoulder a squeeze. "Don't listen to him. I think if anybody at that den of sin has a clue, it's you."

"Thanks. I think?"

The coffee shop owner gave me a pat. "I was in a position like you not too long ago. If it wasn't for Bernard, I would have had to close the doors. You're capable of more than you think. Just make sure you rely on the people around you."

The vote of confidence was appreciated. I came in here a jumble of thoughts about EO, but nothing like impending doom to put your life in perspective. Reaching across the table, I swiped a sausage link off Xander's plate and devoured it before he could protest.

Across the coffee shop, cell phones vibrated. There was only one thing in Vanguard City that warranted an all-points bulletin. As I fished out my cell phone, my suspicions were right. The HeroApp™ had gone crazy. There were multiple names streaming across the app, alerting the populace to their attack on a skyscraper in the business district.

"What the ever-loving-hell?" Griffin mumbled.

Chad turned on the television to Hero News, and the reporters were already on the scene. Zipper sped into the coffee shop, looking for his morning fix of caffeine. The speedster ground to a halt, his hand wrapped around the thermos that waited for him every morning.

"Whoa," I mumbled. For all the years I had been coming to the HideOut, I had never seen the superhero standing still. The skin-tight suit hugged every lean muscle of his body. I had seen him do interviews, but it was almost awkward not seeing the blur of his coming and going.

"Reports are saying the Nocturnals are inside the skyscraper. The group of five supervillains have been on the rise in recent days. There have been no demands, and their intent remains a mystery."

"I need to head out," Bernard said.

"Give 'em hell, Papi." I paused, eyeing the big man. He raised an eyebrow at the same time Griffin kicked my leg under the table. "I assume you'll be giving a public statement when the Centurions save the day?"

"I should head out, too. Somebody is going to need a band-aid." Xander stuffed the last sausage in his mouth, and the two men exited.

"Eventually, we're going to sit him down and have a talk," I said to Griffin.

"There's no 'we' in that conversation," Griffin said.

"It seems they are letting the hostages onto the penthouse terrace. We're counting six of them, but—" The reporter on the

television gasped. *"They're running for the edge of the building."*

Several men in the coffee shop stood up, hands covering their mouths as we watched in horror. One moment Zipper stood next to the counter holding a full thermos of specialty coffee, and the next, the metal container fell where he had been standing. He was fast, but could he make it up the building, past the Nocturnals, and save the hostages before they hurled themselves off the building?

"Don't do it," Griffin whispered, as if the people on the television might listen.

He reached out, lacing his fingers with mine. Nothing about this was unique, or even uncommon. But it was rare that the villains attacked in broad daylight and that we'd watch a televised massacre. Much like Griffin, I had faith that the heroes would come to their rescue, but it didn't lower my anxiety.

"Oh no!" a nearby man yelled.

The reporter in the helicopters swore as a hostage, a woman in business attire, ran at top speed. Without hesitating, she hurled herself off the building. Whatever was going on inside must be terrifying for them to commit suicide. Did they have faith they'd be saved or was this the lesser of two evils?

I held my breath.

"There are no fliers nearby," the reporter said, staring at her cell phone.

One second the jumpers were falling, and then they were nowhere to be found. The reporter leaned out of the helicopter, looking down.

Her eyes went wide. "They're gone."

The cameraman zoomed in to where they had vanished. I recognized the six holes hovering in space before they disappeared.

"EO." I couldn't hide the smirk as it turned into a full grin.

I didn't care if he duked it out with the baddies or if he put them behind bars. Without any credit for himself, EO had saved the lives of six innocent citizens. For that, he'd drink for free tonight. If he showed, that is.

"Our hero chaser is smitten." Griffin laughed.

Who me? Nope. I didn't get smitten. Griffin leaned against me, wrapping his arm around my waist. "It's about time you found a special someone." He was going to be insufferable.

But maybe, just maybe, I didn't mind.

8

───────────

I held my breath every time Bruno opened the door and granted the superhero elite access to the club. So far this evening, my attention to the people entering the Alley caused me to drop a glass, shoot an olive across the room, and poor half a martini on my shoe.

I cost the club enough money that it warranted Scarlet coming to the bar. As she sauntered in my direction, I prepared her gin and tonic, ensuring that her lime was sliced perfectly and given a twist. If I botched her drink, I might not need to worry about the sale of the club. I'd be jobless before the conversation started.

She pulled back a chair, brushing it off before she took a seat. She had pinned her hair back into a bun, letting strands fall along her cheeks. Scarlet never arrived at work in anything less than a full face of makeup. The staff had a running theory that it wasn't cosmetics at all and that she had her face surgically altered. Ordinary people weren't this stunning. But then again, Scarlet wasn't an average human.

"Your gin and tonic, m'lady."

"Don't think you can charm your way into my good graces."

"Me?" I batted my eyelashes. "I would never think to use my God-given talents on somebody as refined as yourself."

She held the drink to her lips before speaking. "Every family has that one person you want to slap." She took a sip, closing her eyes as she savored the perfect concoction. "But they're too damned lovable."

"I have no idea who you're talking about." Scarlet had poached me years ago from a horrible dive bar. Back then, on a good night, I barely made enough to buy myself three meals a day. I always wondered if she used her gifts to lure me away. Every time I asked, she'd give a little shrug and wander back into the crowd.

"What's on your mind?" She didn't beat around the bush.

"Nothing more than usual."

"That's not what Vengeful Mist said as he fished an olive out of his tunic."

"Can a mist be vengeful?"

"Speak." She dragged the word out into two syllables in

an almost sing-song manner. I resisted. Images of puppies and doing my taxes filled my head. But once Scarlet unleashed her gifts, it was impossible to ignore her demands.

"I don't want you to sell the club."

"Is that what's gotten under your skin? There's a good chance I've found a buyer. He fancies himself a hero, but he just wants to hobnob with the A-listers."

"Eclipse," I growled louder than I meant to.

"Yes, Eclipse. He's not much of a hero, but he does like the idea of taking over the club. It'd put him within touching distance of all the important players. The man's vanity should keep Midnight Alley open for years."

"How can you sell it to a man who pretends to be a hero? He'll run the club into the ground, and us with it."

"Aging parents. Multiple mortgages. Crushing debt. Trust me, I don't want to sell the club, but it's the only way I'm going to retire. It's bad enough to see it go. Do you think I want to sell it to him?"

"I've never considered you a villain, but…"

"Alejandro, are you sure you don't have a rich relative? Maybe you were adopted and your actual parents are wealthy jet setters?"

"Mi madre would slap the stupid out of me if I said maybe. If I have to hear how I'm just like my father one more time…"

"Now, are you going to tell me what's really on your mind?"

"I don't know—"

"Speak."

I cursed under my breath. "I'm hoping a specific gentleman shows up tonight."

"Rabid Squirrel?"

"How are chipmunk cheeks a power?"

"Mystery Man?"

"His name is Stewart. He's hardly a mystery."

"The Great—"

"Does the phrase, 'is it in yet' sound great?"

Scarlet whistled before taking another drink. While the other staff might give me grief, she never judged me on my extracurricular activities. She had garnered quite a reputation in her younger years. But as she got older, she questioned if her trysts were because they were into her or because her voice held the ability to sway men. Thankfully, she found a telepath who required no words to communicate.

"What's special about this one?"

I pressed against the bar, gesturing for her to lean closer. "I think he might be a gentleman."

She raised an eyebrow. "Confirmed?"

I nodded. "Strong supporting evidence."

"Well, I'll be damned." She tipped back the drink, polishing off the last of the gin.

"Hero in the street..."

"Villain in the sheets." She bumped fists with me. "I hope you're right, Alejandro. Now stop breaking glasses, or you'll never afford to buy the club."

She had barely vanished into the crowd when somebody coughed behind me. I spun about to see EO's face through a portal separating me from the liquor on the shelves. I was about to ask how long he'd been standing.

"A villain in the sheets, huh?"

Being Mexican meant I could rely on genetics to hide a slight blush. This was anything but slight. I could weave between the admirations of patrons all night, but this man overhears a one-liner between me and the boss lady, and suddenly I felt like a teenager again.

"About that..."

He stepped to the side and vanished from sight. I was about to curse when he cleared his throat from the other side of the bar. I would have to get used to a man who could move in ways that defied the laws of nature. By the time I breathed a sigh of relief, he was pulling out a chair and taking his seat.

"Don't worry," he laughed, "I am."

I raised an eyebrow, unsure of what he meant. The funny expression on his face had me blushing again. Oh, great. He was going to think I was a giddy child, unable to control the rush of blood to his face. It didn't get better when he reached into a portal and pulled out a bouquet of white roses.

"Too much? Are you a flower guy? White seemed appropriate. You know, with you being all pure and stuff."

"You're nervous." Did I just say that out loud? How long had it been since a guy chased me? You'd think this was the first time I ever considered a second date with a man. "I mean, you literally saved half a dozen people from plummeting to their deaths, and you're rambling with *me*?"

"Being a superhero isn't that hard. You follow the playbook and—"

"Wait, is there really a playbook?" I couldn't tell if he was messing with me. Did Griffin know this? If I could get a copy, he'd owe me for life.

"Have you heard of Hellcat? She's brutal when training heroes new to Vanguard. I'm pretty sure I failed my pop quiz yesterday."

He couldn't possibly be serious? The amount of homework they gave the new students would be his next complaint.

"As I was saying. I can save people. It's pretty easy when you just remember that your job is to not let anybody die. Courting a sexy man with an accent, that's a bit more nerve-wracking."

I swiped the flowers out of his hand. It was the first time a man had ever brought me flowers. Although he wore a half leather uniform with a reflective chest plate, his momma brought him up proper. I could appreciate a man with traditional views of courting.

He reached over the counter and pulled one free from the bouquet. "Stonewall is going to give me grief if he doesn't get one."

Traditional-ish.

EO had been laying it on thick enough I nearly forgot that there was another man. No, not another man, his husband. I went from blushing back to trying to understand exactly what was going on here. What was the protocol when Stonewall arrived? Did I act like a mistress and pretend nothing occurred between us? Or did we swap notes about EO's dating techniques?

"You're uncomfortable. I went overboard."

I lifted the flowers to my nose, breathing in their intoxicating scent. Roses had never smelled this sweet. Where in the world had he found them? Paris? Greece? Did he zip to the other side of the globe to run errands?

Finally, I shook my head. "Not uncomfortable. They're sweet. *You're* sweet. I just don't know the rules of this game. Is Stonewall going to be mad? Jealous? Do I act like a handsome man didn't just bring me flowers? I have a lot of questions."

"Aw, you're handsome too." He shimmied forward in his chair, resting his elbows on the counter. "He knows I saved you from the Naga. I told him about going to Paris."

"Oh."

"I didn't tell him we kissed."

"Why?"

His brow furrowed in an adorable manner as he pondered the question. People like Griffin think superheroes were at their sexiest when turning into fire or flying through the city. For me, it was their most basic human characteristics that made them appealing. He could save an airplane from falling out of the sky, but in a casual conversation, three little lines appeared over his head as he struggled to find words.

"That was a moment between us. He doesn't need to know."

"So you're lying to him?"

EO shook his head. "If he asked, I'd gladly tell him. I told him about Paris because I didn't want him to be worried. You might not know this, but I'm in a dangerous line of work."

"And here I thought it was all signing photographs and kissing babies."

"Would you feel more comfortable if I told him?" he asked.

It was a loaded question. Thankfully, a couple raised a hand further down the bar. It'd give me a couple minutes to process a sea of uncertainties. I took my time as I grabbed their beers, slowly popping off the caps. I almost offered them a house cocktail just so I could dwell further. My lackluster performance netted me a single dollar for a tip. I deserved it.

"I don't want to be your dirty secret."

"Let me ask you this. Do you want to know about the last time Stone and I had sex? Cause I could tell you about the—"

I held up my hands in protest. "I get it. Wow, never thought I'd stop somebody from telling me about getting busy in the bedroom."

"Chernobyl."

"What?"

"The bedroom is so tame."

My cock jumped at the prospect of sex without geographical limitations. He had a point. Part of me was turned on at the idea of him with his husband, but I didn't need to know the details, despite my little friend's objections.

"What if he asks?"

"He might at some point. And if you're okay with it, I'll tell him."

"If I'm not?" I didn't want to be difficult. Bringing home a superhero and knocking boots meant the most complicated part was deciding between silicone or water-based lube. Part of this conversation was refreshing, hearing a man open to having a dialogue even if the conversations got difficult. However, it also felt as if it was a maze of feelings that needed navigating.

"I'd ask him to respect that," EO said with confidence. He held his arm across the bar, palm up, waiting for me to offer mine.

I felt stupid asking. Of course, he and Stonewall had talked about this before they decided to date outside their marriage. I'd be the first to admit that I wasn't great at the emotional side of relationships. Sex was just sex. But in a relationship, there were feelings. But I liked knowing he could express those with his partner.

"It sounds like this might be too much for you."

He started to retreat when I grabbed his hand. "Maybe." I gave his hand a firm squeeze. "Just be patient."

He lingered, his thumb running back and forth across my knuckles. Scarlet didn't mind me fraternizing with the patrons, but if I didn't start slinging cocktails, she'd escort EO out the door herself. I had given Griffin a hard time about treating Sebastian as his everything. How could one man be your one and only? But EO and Stonewall were showing me it wasn't the only option.

"I need to get back to work before Scarlet fires me. But later, you're going to explain why you chose Chernobyl."

Even as I let go of his hand and stashed the roses behind the bar, I could still feel his thumb caressing the valley between my knuckles. A muscle deep in the pit of my stomach tightened and doubled down when I thought about kissing the hero. Fine, I admit it. I was smitten.

9

Stonewall had more muscle than should be feasible. On the HeroApp™, it classified him as a "bruiser." It meant that most of his powers came from the fact he was strong beyond measure. He barely fit into the booth on the side of the club, and I was convinced that if he flexed, the spandex suit would tear off his frame.

Midnight Alley had a very different feeling when the lights came on. It went from sexy and sultry to sexy and blinding. The velvet walls lost their lush qualities, and the uncanny number of glasses and bottles littering the tables were almost too many to count.

EO's husband had arrived minutes before last call. I didn't have the heart to turn him away, especially when EO had vanished to help stop a crisis in the Australian Outback. Scarlet tried to cite club policy, but she bowed out of the conversation when I commented on being distraught over the sale of the club. I would have to use that more often to get out of crappy shifts. For now, the bar had been reset and I could catch my breath with Stonewall.

He sipped his beer quietly, admiring the club from his perch. I had looked him up on the HeroApp™, and there were plenty of photos of him in action. The man had a knack for getting into the middle of a fray and throwing fists with the best of them. I imagined at this rate, he'd be tapped on the shoulder to join a team.

On my way to his table, I grabbed chairs, flipping them upside down on tables to make life easier for the cleaning staff. It gave me a few extra seconds to think about what I was going to say. The night had been non-stop heroes celebrating a victory over Atlantis and another attempt to enslave mankind. It meant I had little time to exchange pleasantries with EO as the night carried on. But now that it was empty, I figured I'd face EO's husband.

"I kissed your husband." Impulse control was in the column of traits I needed to work on. I bit my lip, waiting for him to jump to his feet. If he slapped me, I'm pretty sure he'd send me through a wall. Please, please, please, don't hit the face. It's my money maker.

With his cowl hiding most of his face and his eyes coated in black paint, it was difficult to read his reaction. He held the single white rose in his right hand, and I half expected him to snap the stem before throwing a table at me. Bruno might be strong, but he'd never win this arm-wrestling contest.

"I figured."

"You knew?" I asked.

"He came home with a goofy grin on his face. He's not really good at keeping secrets."

"Not how I expected this conversation to go."

"He mentioned you were nervous. Normally, I'd keep my nose out of his business and let him do his thing. But there is something you need to know."

I slid into the booth opposite the big man. I prepared for him to get territorial, to throw a heap of rules on the table and expect me to abide by his expectations. I had been in threesomes like that before. When sex required a referee, it lost its zeal.

"I'm okay with this. Let me put it like this. EO loves horror movies. I hate them. Give me a rom-com any day of the week. He'll ask me if I want to go to the theater and see people get killed on screen. I always say no. But I don't tell him not to see it. And why do it alone? Take a friend who loves horror."

"Wait, am I the horror-loving friend in this example?"

Stonewall laughed hard enough that he shifted the table. It was a long night, and I needed some clarity, so I didn't want to misinterpret his analogy. The roar continued, and I had to stop and smile. He wiped his eyes, smearing the paint inside his mask.

"You're definitely his movie buddy."

"Are there rules for attending this theater?"

"Be honest. Be you. You might have noticed we're pretty big on this communication thing."

"What about you and me?"

He cocked his head to the side before his eyes went wide. "Oh, you mean you and me like *you and me*. You're not my type."

"Oh thank God."

"Whoa, now. You're going to bruise my ego."

To see a man his size offended by my lack of interest bordered on comical. With muscles like that, he could very well have any man he wanted. I suspected half the muscle was from beating the men off with a stick.

"Of course, we're still fairly new to town. Local friends wouldn't hurt either."

He held his hand across the table. I reached out tentatively, prepared for him to grind my bones into a fine powder. He gave it a shake, almost delicate.

"Nice to meet you, Alejandro."

"Same to you, Mr. Wall."

He laughed. For all my worries, a simple chuckle put them at ease.

At least we had something other than EO in common. "About these rom-coms? Did you see *Forever My Disaster*?"

The man slapped the table, nearly knocking over his beer. He leaned over the table, the excitement barely contained. He definitely loved his rom-coms with that kind of reaction.

"Why did Monica go with him? She should have stayed with Ted."

I waggled my finger back and forth. "Nope. I'm team Vinny. Those two are going to have adorable babies."

"If she had been smart, she'd have taken them both. Ladies are into spit roasting, right?"

"I mean, who isn't?"

The argument continued for the next half hour as we jumped from one movie to the next. Apparently, I'd be watching rom-coms and horror movies in this scenario. Leave it to two gay men to bond over sappy love stories. I realized I could very well be living one now. Was this the beginning of my own rom-com? ¡Cielos! I was going to be annoyed if the scene faded to black when I dragged EO back to my apartment.

Now that I thought about it, yeah, that needed to happen.

10

———————

The subway of Vanguard City might as well have a welcome mat laid out for villains. The station closest to Midnight Alley hadn't been renovated in twenty years, and it'd be any day before they condemned it. Between the flickering fluorescent bulbs and the tiles falling off the columns along the platform, it screamed evil lair.

At this hour, the trains were infrequent, and there was a good chance I'd be waiting for the next thirty minutes. That's about twenty-nine minutes longer than I wanted to be there. Between the muggy smell of decay and the rats scurrying into the shadows, it was almost a guarantee that a superpowered psycho would show and take me hostage.

It wouldn't be the first time, nor the last.

The digital sign above the platform had the arrival time except that enough of the bulbs were blown that I couldn't tell if it was twenty minutes or fifty. I considered speeding back through the turnstile and up to the street and calling a taxi. It'd be worth the twenty bucks to not have the hair on my arms standing on end.

A glass bottle clanked against the ground somewhere nearby. I spun about, looking both ways down the long corridor. There were plenty of alcoves for somebody to hide, and the columns casting shadows made for the perfect supervillain entrance.

"Here we go," I mumbled. I just wanted to go home and crawl into bed. Instead, I was going to be granted a supervillain monologue, a long-winded plan for world domination, and an elaborate plan with far too many holes for success.

"Is anybody there?" The best villains didn't lure their victims into a false sense of security; they struck whenever it suited them. But the B-rate villains, it was almost as if they had watched one too many cartoons. Griffin had started working on a book about the comical situations created by villains. I'd have to carry a copy so I could hand it out. Vanguard City deserved better villains.

"I guess I'm alone." When I turned around, there'd be a man standing there, hoping to surprise me. Predictable.

When I turned around, there were only shadows where I expected to see a latex body suit. Could it be my paranoia? Had I been listening to Griffin too long? Maybe his book—

The lights above flared, bursting until only a single

bulb remained. I shielded my eyes as sparks erupted from the ceiling. Dammit, I had fallen right into their trap. When I looked again, the shadows moved into the light, forming the shape of a man. He stepped out, clad in a white leather suit and cape. Most suits that showed the eyes or mouth for practical reasons, but he had white fabric covering his face, leaving him featureless.

"White Knight?"

His head shook side-to-side, slow, deliberate. I couldn't think of any other superpowered people that preferred a monochrome suit. The lack of words or movement was almost as eerie as not being able to read his expression. Behind him, four other figures appeared from the shadows. It was the group that had been terrorizing the city for the last few weeks.

"I'll be—"

As a wall of cool covered my skin, I didn't have a smart-ass comment. I looked down, expecting to see a mist or cloud brushing against my hands, but nothing in the station moved. The temperature dropped, causing a shiver. My heart raced, and I could barely keep my breathing under control.

"What's happening?"

"Fear." The raspy voice fit the featureless face.

I had gone into the subway and nobody knew where I was. When this brightly dressed villain killed me, my body wouldn't be found until the next day when the commuters returned. Bernard could see my location, but he was probably busy. No, he didn't care enough to break away from his precious Centurions to save somebody as insignificant as me.

"I can taste your fear."

Was that his power? To induce fear? It was hard to concentrate when the overwhelming sadness of a funeral with no attendees crossed my mind. Mi mamá wouldn't leave Mexico City to bury her only son. It'd be proof that nobody in life cared about me. What a way to start my eternal afterlife.

Dead before I could get EO naked. Not that it would happen. As much as I liked the guy, I was being used to patch up something in his relationship. No matter how hard he and Stonewall tried to convince me, I'd just be a third wheel in their relationship. Used. In their twisted game, I understood neither of them cared for me.

"I'm alone," I whispered.

"Yes," the man in white hissed.

What was the point? My love life was in shambles, and with Scarlet selling the bar, I had nothing. I didn't want to continue this slow spiral to oblivion. With the sound of the subway train heading toward the station, I made a decision. I wouldn't be alone anymore. I simply wouldn't be.

The cold had penetrated my skin. My temperature had dropped, forcing me to hug myself. But even the man's powers didn't compare to the cold dark hole growing inside my heart. I couldn't focus on anything other than the over-whelming sense of sadness causing tears to stream down my face.

"It's the only answer."

The man in white was right. I didn't have the will to endure this any longer. I raced toward the ledge. There was no hesitation as I hopped down, landing on the wooden slats connecting the rails. I squared off against the light at the end of the tunnel. The loneliness would only last a few more seconds and then I'd be done with it.

Shouting erupted from the platform. I could barely see over the ledge, but it was enough to see a woman in purple leather holding a long, slender staff. I'd met Hellcat at the Alley more than once, and her tenacity was legendary. Even without powers, the heroes respected her. I wish I had garnered even a fraction of the admiration she received.

She brought down the staff on the man in white. He blocked her strike, but she was already spinning about, the heel of her foot knocking his face to the side. One-on-one, she might have stood a chance. But with the man's cronies nearby, the powerless vigilante would be hard pressed to walk away unscathed.

The ground rumbled as the train approached. My time was coming to an end. It'd only be a matter of seconds before the pain vanished. It'd be a second of pain, and then I'd be free.

"EO, I need an evac."

Hellcat lunged from the ledge. Her arm snaked around my chest, and in a feat of martial arts, she swung around, standing behind me. Three seconds and I'd be gone, and unfortunately, so would Hellcat.

"EO, now!"

The air vibrated as the train sped into the station. The light grew until it was blinding. Screeching filled the air, causing more tiles to shower from the station ceiling. The conductor attempted to save my life, but it was too late.

The nothing swallowed us both.

11

I screamed.

I threw my hands in front of me, expecting the train to smash me into tiny bits. There was no light in the space. Turning my head mid-scream, I could feel something soft touching my cheek. I patted the surrounding space, surprised to find soft fabric instead of the cold hard steel of the train.

The last thing I remembered was standing on the platform. No, I had gotten onto the tracks, wanting to stop the pain. The pain? My brain was a jumble of thoughts, from the breakfast crew to my funeral. What had happened on that platform?

The man in white.

It came rushing in. The Nocturnals appeared on the platform, and before I knew it, I was hurling myself in front of a subway car. I remembered the people on the skyscraper throwing themselves to their death. It all made sense now. The man in white did something. Did he have some ability to draw out his victim's worse fears?

Leaning back, I rested a hand on my chest, to the steady pounding of my heart.

"Where am—"

The darkness shrank as a door opened, light flooding the room, *my* room. Standing in the doorway, I could see the outline of a man. The sparkling glint from the uniform gave away his identity. EO had come to my rescue. It was becoming the foundation of our relationship.

"You were shouting. Is everything okay?"

The light pouring in was brighter than a lightbulb. I had been out cold long enough for the sun to rise. Nothing made sense. All I wanted to do was curl into a ball and pull the blankets over my head. I appreciated him saving me, but something in my heart hurt and I wanted to be alone.

"It'll be a little while before his powers wear off."

"Thanks," I whispered. I don't think the words quite did the situation justice. He had saved me from a snake, a jerk at the bar, a horrible date experience, and now he swooped in and protected me against myself. Thanks didn't quite seem to convey my appreciation.

"What happened? I remember—"

"Hellcat happened. She's two parts fearless, one part

crazy. She had a hunch that something was going to happen tonight. Nobody dies on her watch."

"The train?"

"I teleported the two of you out just in time. I thought you'd be more comfortable in your own bed while you slept off his powers."

"Thanks."

"You already said that."

With the light behind him, I couldn't make out his face. But I imagined the crooked grin growing. The man in white had reached into my brain and weaponized my worst fears. I hadn't realized how much it ate at me. I had great friends, a decent job, and with this bear of a man in my doorway, there were possibilities. But some part of me expected them to walk away and leave me alone.

"I'll be out here if you need me."

Always the gentleman, EO turned around, ready to close the door. It might be the villain's powers, but space was the last thing I needed. The feeling of dread was like rising waters, and if I didn't get a lifeline, I wasn't sure I'd survive.

My lifeline pulled the door closed.

"Don't."

"I can leave it open."

"Don't go."

He paused.

I fought back tears. He had gone above and beyond.

First, he saved me, and then he stood as a vigilant protector. Despite that, here I was with an even bigger ask. I could hardly make sense of the emotions causing my heart to tighten. But one thing was for certain, I didn't want the man who brought me roses to leave.

"Are you sure? You almost died... again. That can make a person—"

I cleared my throat. "I want you to stay."

He walked closer as I sat up in bed. I crawled to my knees, looking up at him as he stood at the side of the bed. The moment my hand touched his neck, it became clear that I needed this. Be damned the villain's powers. I needed to feel EO.

He dipped down, lips crushing against mine. Holding the sides of my head, there was an eagerness to his actions. His beard brushed against my stubble. The taste of cinnamon hit me as if it were an intoxicating aphrodisiac. As he backed away, teeth pulling at my bottom lip, I didn't want to stop, not there.

"EO," I whispered in a breathy gasp, "that suit would look better on the floor."

He chuckled at my poor excuse for a pickup line. Resting his forehead against mine, he wrapped his arms around my chest, pulling me tight for a hug. The man's strength chased away the dark thoughts. He kissed my forehead before giving me another squeeze.

"Theo."

"What?"

"My name," he whispered, "it's Theodore."

I couldn't help but laugh. Superheroes had a long list of reasons for the monikers they picked. Most used it to strike fear into their villains. Others treated them as descriptors for their powers. But this was the first time I heard of a hero using a childhood nickname.

I pulled back, running a hand down his thick beard. "Nice to meet you, Theodore."

"Oh no," he shook his head. "Only my mom calls me that."

"Well, if it's good enough for your mom—"

"I don't want to think about her while you call my name."

My cock jumped at the confirmation that this was foreplay. I had imagined him naked, but to strip him out of his suit, the fabric tightened across my groin.

"Theo it is."

———

Theo didn't *just* take off his suit. He danced.

"Are you doing a striptease?" At the foot of the bed, it was like watching the drunk straight men at the club jamming out to the songs of their youths. I knew a train wreck when I saw one, but I couldn't look away as they relived their glory days.

"Irresistible, right?"

"I can't do this," I protested. Holding up a finger, he paused his gyrating hips. I pulled the phone out of my pocket and flipped to my bedroom playlist. What? I like to be prepared for sexy times. I plugged the phone into the stand next to my bed, and the music filled the bedroom.

"Now?" he asked.

"Now." I nodded, lying back on the bed in nothing but boxer briefs. If I had kept my clothes on, I'd have returned the favor.

He was a horrible dancer. Not just bad, but if it were any other man, it'd have been laughable. But Theo's confidence had its own appeal. There was no arrogance, just a sense of pride in everything he did. While I might want to strip him naked, his thick body remained his *second* sexiest trait.

Turning to the side, he tossed in a pelvic thrust that didn't quite line up with the music. Reaching to his side, he unfastened the snaps holding his armor in place. I held my breath as he did a side step, pulling the chest plate over his head. He was as bearish as they came. The armor hid soft padding with just a hint of muscle, but from the chest down, every inch of his body was covered in hair.

I whistled.

He tossed the armor to the side, but it never hit the floor, vanishing through a portal. I heard a thud in the living room. I had almost forgotten the sexy beast seducing me had this incredible power. Now, if only he could make his pants vanish.

My prayers were answered as he turned, letting me get a clear view of his ass. The leather pants were painted on and required effort to peel down his body. Inch-by-inch, I got the chance to see... a jock?

"¡Santos Dios!"

By the time his suit reached his knees, he had turned. There was no holding back as he raised his arms, thrusting his hips as he gave into the music. It was less of a striptease at this point and more of a poorly choreographed flash mob. But he meant this show just for me, and it was impossible to hide my excitement.

I laughed as he paused his dance moves to kick off his boots. Hopping on one foot, he wrestled with his pants. Thankfully, it had been a Nagatine that attacked two nights ago, because if it had been his pants, I'm pretty sure we'd both be dead. With one last kick, they flew across the room, vanishing into a portal and landing somewhere in the living room.

He leaned forward as if he was about to crawl onto the bed, but I wasn't having that. "Uh no. I didn't watch that for you to end when it got good."

"Snared by my sexy?"

Dammit, he wasn't wrong. How did he manage to be this charming? "I'm not hating it."

I got to my knees and crawled closer as he treated me

to… the Electric Slide? If it wasn't for him flexing and his package bouncing, I'd have turned on the lights and sent him on the hunt for a bachelorette party. I reached the end of the mattress. He was close enough for me to be impressed by the bulge of his jock.

When my finger hooked on his waistband, he slowed his moves. With only two sheer pieces of fabric between us, he kept a devilish smile plastered on his face. But his eyes, they didn't have an ounce of humor in them. I had seen the expression a hundred times before as a man realized he was seconds from having his cock touched.

He robbed me of a hard-won victory as his hands vanished into portals. Hands rested on the back of my shoulders and pulled me back onto the bed. I tried to sit up, but another portal appeared above me. His hand rested on my chest. As he got onto the bed, he crawled over me, kissing up my thigh. He paused as he reached for my underwear, leaning in close to the tent, letting me feel his breath before he left a trail up my torso. He licked my nipple before resting on his elbows on top of me.

"You're a horrible dancer," I laughed.

"I'm hurt," he jested. "I'll just take my sick dance moves and go home and write in my diary. Dear Diary—"

I kissed Theo. He made up for what he lacked in rhythm with his ability to kiss. It was the perfect mix of pressure, tongue, and even teeth. If he hadn't trapped my cock between us, suffering from friction burn in my underwear, I'd never want him to stop. I could live in this moment, the taste of him lingering on my lips.

"Are you hiding a lead pipe?" He reached down and gave my cock a squeeze, and my hips bucked.

Every partner in the bedroom had a personality. Some are serious and dead set on working toward a sweaty finale. Others are passive and like to lay back and be serviced. Theo, however, was a mix of boyish humor that weaved in and out of desire. Even if we called it quits, this had already exceeded my expectations.

Let me be clear. I did *not* want to call it quits.

He rocked back onto his knees and tugged my underwear down. Unpredictable. I didn't know if he'd wrap his fingers around it or slap it around like a kitten with a ball of yarn. He laid across my body, kissing the spot just beneath my navel. As he reached my cock, his beard brushed against my cock as he gently kissed my balls. If only his dancing had this level of skill.

"Excited?" Did he really just ask that?

Before I replied, he dragged his tongue up the length of my shaft, licking until he reached the head of my cock, peaking from my foreskin. As he eased the skin back, it glistened. Delicately, he ran his tongue around the head, licking the precum clean. He hovered for a moment, kissing the head, teasing.

"You're killing me." The words came out as desperate. He replied by swallowing my cock, taking the first few inches in his mouth before retreating. On the third go, he reached the base and held his head in place, determined to take every inch.

I reached back, grabbing the pillow as I tried to hold my hips in place. When he grabbed my hips, fingers digging into the flesh of my ass, he continued up and down the length of my cock. I nearly lost it.

"Keep that up—"

The universal cue translated to, "If you want this to end now, keep doing what you're doing." Part of me wanted to come, to feel my cock in the back of his throat as I let the orgasm curl my toes. He held my cock against my belly as he licked my sack. It was heaven… then he moved lower, pushing my knees toward my chest. His tongue ran along the skin between my ass and balls and leaving a trail that felt like electricity.

"Not helping," I begged.

"Whachumeannothelpin," he muttered as his tongue grazed my ass. I squealed, the pillow in my hand dangerously close to being torn apart.

Lowering my legs, he crawled along my body. A more carnal desire had replaced the boyish charm. When his groin brushed against mine, there was no doubt he was enjoying himself. I thought he'd come in for a kiss, but his lips barely grazed mine. He continued inching his way forward until his legs straddled my chest.

His cock strained against the fabric of his jock. He

leveled it with my face. I was even more excited that he had taken charge. When he pulled the fabric to the side, it surprised me to see a cock that'd require two hands and still leave enough to lick.

I slid my arms under his legs, gripping his ass as I guided him toward my mouth. Unlike him, I didn't have any patience. I wanted him in my mouth. This handsome man who worked so hard to chase away my fears deserved the absolutely best blowjob.

My mouth watered as I wrapped my lips around the head of his cock. Pulling his hips forward, I held my breath, letting it push against the back of my mouth and hit the bend in my throat. His body shivered as he held me in place. Just as I thought I might run out of air, he pulled back.

He continued the slow and steady motion, each time holding just long enough that I had to work to control my breathing. Theo knew his length was a challenge, and a part of him was getting off on making me work for it. But when I pulled a hand from under him and wrapped it around his balls, he lost his pace, shoving all the way down my throat.

"Oh God," he gasped.

I could feel the muscles in his ass tense, a tell-tale sign he was enjoying the servicing. At that point, he sped up, focusing on the last few inches of his cock. Every third stroke, he'd change the pace and then resume the quick tempo. His pacing grew erratic, and I could tell he would not keep up the pace for long. Right now, I wanted to swallow all of Theo and taste him as he came.

A hand reached around my shaft, causing me to gag on his cock. As he pulled out, I could see his face, a smirk flashing before he lost himself again. His arm was cut off at the elbow, buried in a portal, giving him access to my cock. If people wanted to know why I loved sex with superheroes, this answered every question.

He worked the skin over the head of my cock, giving me short, quick strokes, nearly matching the motion of his hips. His ass tightened, and a growl started in the pit of his stomach. It was almost primal as he shoved the length of his cock down my throat. His balls tightened as his shaft thickened, pulsing as he came.

I almost didn't get to appreciate the volume of cum as the tingling in my balls spread throughout my groin and tickled my spine. I thrust my hips into his hand, unable to growl with my mouth full. The warm liquid pelted my stomach enough that I was impressed with myself.

Theo rocked backward, freeing his cock from my mouth. I panted, savoring the warmth flowing through my body. He pulled his hand from the portal before licking his fingers clean. I appreciated a man who didn't waste a good thing.

He laid down next to me, throwing an arm over my

chest. Nuzzling my neck, his beard tickled my chest. The closeness was the sweet end to a sweaty time.

"So much better than your dancing."

"Dear Diary, he doesn't appreciate my interpretive dance."

I kissed his forehead before wiggling closer. Theo had skillfully pushed aside my insecurities caused by the leader of the Nocturnals. The sex had been great, but it was his arm across my chest and leg tangled with mine that chased away the darkness.

"Staying?" I asked. Normally, this would be when I'd complain about being crowded and give them a slap on the ass as they headed to the door. With Theo, I didn't want him to move from that spot.

"If you want me to."

"You sure he won't mind?"

"He knows I'm doing my heroic duties." His voice trailed off, growing quiet as he spoke. "Julian can call if he needs..." He was asleep before he finished the sentence.

I'd be sticky when I woke, but it'd serve as a reminder of how the morning had gone from horrible to magical. I gave him another kiss on the forehead, listening to the steady in and out of his breathing. Leaning my face against his, I followed suit, drifting off to sleep, safe in the arms of a handsome bear.

12

———

I CHECKED THE TIME ON MY PHONE. NEARLY THREE IN THE afternoon, and I found myself sitting outside a posh cafe on the rich side of town. I shifted my seat, trying to use the narrow umbrella to block the sun. I'm sure if Chad saw me, he'd have a heart attack and claim I betrayed him. Baristas were so melodramatic.

The server stopped at my table wearing a button-down maroon dress shirt with a black tie and apron. It looked incredibly stuffy, and before he opened his mouth to take my order, I longed for Chad who knew my order before I spoke. He'd see me walking in the door and by the time I sat down in my usual seat, there'd be a cup of coffee and a bagel.

"May I take your order, sir?"

"Spicy whatever you have. Hold the sir."

He raised his eyebrow, unsure how to process the order. I might as well have been speaking Spanish. "Surprise me."

As he walked away, Bernard appeared, pausing the man to deliver his order. I woke up this morning, sad to find Theo had vanished at some point in the middle of the night. I didn't have time to dwell on it when I received a cryptic message from our den father. It had been a couple weeks since I spent quality time with him outside of the breakfast club. This meetup was long overdue.

"¡Papi!"

His ever stoic face, framed by a bushy beard, faltered. I always enjoyed watching the lines on his forehead deepen while his eyes narrowed. Bernard didn't have a mean bone in his body, but watching him get moody was one of life's little treats.

"No."

"What do you mean, Papi? I can't imagine Papi telling his favorite person no. Isn't that right, Papi?"

I batted my eyelashes while he sighed and shook his head. The amusing part was, even without his armor, massive axe, or the ability to summon lightning, he could still reach across the table and knock me halfway across the city. But for all that power packed into this hirsute man, he was still a teddy bear.

"Okay, I promise to behave."

"Don't make promises we both know you can't keep."

The server returned with a tray and two fancy white

mugs. Setting them down, he vanished before either of us could ask about the sugar or cream. I took a tentative sip, testing the temperature.

"Pumpkin spice? Really? It's not even fall."

"Basic bitches, am I right?" Bernard looked away as he took a swig. I nearly spit out the coffee at his zinger.

"So why did you drag my butt out of bed? I was having such a good dream."

"Something bugged me about yesterday, and I didn't want to bring it up in front of Griffin and Xander."

"I swear, I didn't do it."

He raised an eyebrow. "What?"

"Sorry." I went back to my coffee, trying to not enjoy the delicious nectar with a hint of cinnamon. "Force of habit."

"Are you doing okay?"

That was the million-dollar question. I just had an amazing night of sex and fell asleep next to a beautiful man. There was a hero keeping an eye on me, making sure I wasn't getting in trouble. Scarlet selling the club? That wasn't so great, but it was hard to focus on that right now.

"I don't like the idea of having to find another job. Nothing will ever be as good as the Alley. I mean, maybe I could stay on with the new owner. But it won't be the same."

"It's too bad you can't buy it."

It was the second time becoming the owner had been suggested. The thought of that much responsibility, being in charge of a staff and ensuring they were paid, made me hot under the collar. It could also be the scorching heat and this puny umbrella's inability to actually block the light.

"Sculpture park?" Bernard asked.

"If this is another attempt to force some culture on me—"

"I'm sure you're used to having things forced in you."

My face turned red. I finished the coffee, ignoring the burn as I was overwhelmed with the taste of autumn.

"Yeah, that's what I thought."

He pulled out money, leaving it on the table. I added a few extra dollars for that jerk server surprising me with the most divine coffee possible. Yes, I'm a proud basic bitch.

We walked down the block, in-between the numerous high rises in this part of the city. Most of the people coming and going wore fine suits or fancy dresses. It wasn't quite exquisite enough for a night at the Alley, but it would be close. I felt out of place in my shorts and t-shirt, but at least I wasn't sweating my balls off.

There was a break in the buildings, stopping the steel and concrete and trading it in for vibrant trees. The sculpture park was several blocks in each direction, filled with greenery to give workers something to do on their lunch break. The walkway wound through the park, eventually opening up to a large metal sculpture with ample seating for employees to admire while scarfing down food.

"I wish the Ward had a park like this," I admitted.

"You mean East Park isn't enough?"

"Only if you're looking to get stabbed." Something about the man's demeanor was off. An emergency text and now strolling through the city. I half expected Griffin and Xander waiting to surprise me with an intervention.

"What's going on with you? You're—"

"Paris?"

"Oh. That."

I was still processing what it all meant. Hell, I wasn't entirely sure there was going to be anything between Theo and me. It was hard enough to juggle my feelings for him with my insecurities about him having a bruiser for a husband. I hadn't lied about the situation, but I might have omitted the truth.

"Wait, how did you—"

"Find Friends on your phone. At first, I thought it was broken. But when you're shagging superheroes, nothing shocks me."

"Are you shagging—"

"Don't try and change the subject. What's going on?"

I stared at a statue as I collected my thoughts. Two reflective metal columns were wound about one another. It almost appeared as if two people were hugging, tightly intertwined. It made me think of how I fell asleep this morning. What I wouldn't give to be in bed with Theo right now. I froze when I caught Bernard staring at me.

"You already know, don't you."

"Maybe."

"I met somebody. Well, not met. He saved me from a snake. Well, she was part snake. Then he came to the club. He stuck up for me when a patron was being a jerk. He's sweet. He's confident. Did I mention he's sexy? That's important. Then a taxi drive. Wow, that went wrong. Then he teleported me to Paris. It was beautiful. He was beautiful. Then he brought me flowers. But oh yeah, I nearly get killed by the Nocturnals."

Bernard raised his hand to interject.

"Don't worry, I didn't die. But then there was this fear thing. I can't explain it. But we had sex. It was amazing."

Bernard blinked, and I could see the smoke billowing from his ears. Hopefully, he understood why I had kept it to myself over breakfast. It wasn't a quick conversation, even if I blurted out the whole thing.

"Why didn't you tell us?"

"He's married."

"Cheater?"

I shook my head. "His husband is a nice guy. He encouraged me to go out with him."

"So they're poly?"

I threw my hands up in the air. "¡Joder! How am I the only person that didn't know this was a thing?" I paused my tirade, letting my eyes narrow as I studied Bernard's stoic face. "Wait, how do *you* know?"

"I dated two married men for a while."

"Bernard, to puta."

"You're sounding a little unsure about it."

"Can I have fuzzy feelings about a man that isn't mine?" It sounded foolish to say it out loud. It was like I was a child again learning about relationships from the big kids.

"If a man said you were his, what would you say?"

"I don't belong to anybody."

"What were you asking Griffin about Sebastian moving in?"

I grumbled. "How can one person be your everything?"

"Karma owed you a favor and the universe delivered."

Dammit. Bernard had a point.

The sculpture had a taunting quality, as if it knew I was thinking about my legs wrapped around Theo. He had buried his face against the back of my neck with his hand snaked around my chest. His breathing had turned to snoring, quiet, but enough I knew he'd fallen asleep. Much like the art, I wanted to find myself tangled with the man. At the bottom, I caught the artist's name and the title. It was the sign I needed.

"Comfort in his arms," I whispered.

Bernard grabbed me about the waist, pulling me close enough that I had to hold onto him. Resting my head on his shoulder, I wanted to kiss his cheek and say thank you. But with Bernard, you didn't need to voice the words. His eyes always held a shimmer that said he knew his worth. I envied him and the way he walked through life with such certainty.

"What about you, Mr. Castle? Is there a man?"

"Once upon a time."

Bernard never talked about the men he was dating. He spoke openly about every aspect of his life that I assumed there wasn't anybody. Even Xander shrugged when asked. I was ready to jump and click my heels as I shoved aside my insecurities, and I wanted the same for him.

"The one that got away?"

"Something like that," he said, neither confirming nor denying.

"I think it's time to fix that."

"Maybe."

"If karma owes me a favor, it's in your debt, Papi. The whole city is."

"Why do you—" Bernard leaned back, studying my face. There were many times when he'd shoot me a curious glance when one of my stories got too outlandish for even him. But this time, he attempted to take inventory. I made sure my eyebrow rose far enough that it bordered on comical. He had opened the door for this conversation and I was going to push my luck.

"You—"

"Yup."

"How?"

"Doesn't matter."

He scowled.

"We're going to need to talk." He had broken out the dad voice.

"Talk about what?" I raised my shoulders, playing innocent.

"Alejandro."

"We can talk right after you tell me about this missed opportunity."

The rest of the world might see a smart-mouthed bartender always talking about his latest conquest. But if there was one thing I wanted to be for those around me, it was a friend. Theo could wait. If anybody would understand needing to take care of existing relationships, it'd be him. For now, Bernard had a story that needed hearing. Then we could celebrate his affinity for spandex.

"His name was Jason..."

13

———

No villains. No meteor heading to Earth. No ancient race of sentient fish. With no titanic battles to celebrate, the club turned into a dull night of patrons rubbing elbows. I debated going home and breaking out my chaps and cape just to drum up some action. Heroes tipped better when they were regaling one another with their tales of bravery.

"Scarlet," I whined. "Can you do your thing and make them drink? They don't need to get drunk, but if one more person asks for a Diet Coke with a cherry, I might go find some radioactive spiders."

"Alejandro, are we doing this again?"

"Don't tell me you haven't bewitched people before for your amusement. This whole with great power—"

"*My* amusement," she said with a smile. "Wouldn't you like to know how useful this can be in the bedroom?" She ran her hands up her chest to her neck, humming as she put on a show. I had never taken the opportunity to crawl into bed with a woman before, but for Scarlet, my sexuality would turn fluid.

Scarlet let out a laugh, leaning over the bar, and patting me on the cheek. "You couldn't handle this, Alejandro."

"I'm sure. But it'd be fun to try."

She sat back on her stool, pushing her glass across the counter. "Another Diet Coke, two cherries." Just to emphasize the cruelty, her power drifted into the words. Even if I wanted to throw a tantrum, I'd have to do it while my body betrayed me.

"I hate you."

She locked eyes as she brought the straw to her lips. Puckering, she took a long swig. I knew it was a show, but my penis wasn't sure if he should be excited or scared. No, no, be scared little guy. She'd break you. It ended with her fishing out a cherry, carefully pulling it from the stem with her tongue.

"You're going to miss the Alley, aren't you?"

"You know why I bought this place?"

"Cause the building was condemned?"

Scarlet ignored my joke. "The first time Corvid put on the suit, she found a woman wandering the streets barefoot. This poor lady had been kidnapped and with no family, nobody came to her rescue. She was one of twelve women held captive."

Scarlet never talked about her time as a hero. What little I knew came from water cooler gossip. But like so many heroes, she held that gaze that cut through time and space to recount all the things she *should* have done differently. I couldn't imagine the sultry vixen as a masked crusader.

"I found them. Undesirables. They were terrified. But that night, I made the world a better place."

"You found them here?"

Her laugh was like gentle bells filling the room. "No, you dolt. Afterward, Corvid went to the bar to celebrate. But I had to keep it a secret, and that nearly did me in. She, *I,* made the world a better place. I helped people. But I couldn't share it with anybody."

"This was the bar."

She nodded as she took another sip. "And this is the same spot where I reminded myself if I was going to keep saving lives, I needed to keep my secret. When I retired the mask, I decided these blowhards needed a place to let off some steam from carrying the burden of the world."

The tabloids made it sound as if Midnight Alley was nothing more than an elite club for heroes. While we catered to a specific clientele, it served a necessary purpose for so many.

"I wish you didn't need to sell."

"If I had my way, I'd gift it to you and Bruno. Then you could hire an over-sexed bartender and poetic bouncer.

Then you'd see the pains in the ass you've been. But I need the money."

I shook my head before I grabbed her empty glass. I refilled it and added two more cherries. "No apologies. You've done a lot for this community, for all of Vanguard. You've earned a cabana on the beach. I'll keep hoping I stumble onto a sugar daddy."

"Stumble is the only thing you won't be doing to that daddy."

"Did I overhear you two talking about my future investment?"

Eclipse and his goon squad. It was bad enough I had to stare at the face of a man dressed in a neatly pressed white suit. But his clones? They were a whole different level of pathetic. So many white outfits and not an ounce of dirt or spray of blood. Either they had the best dry cleaners in Vanguard, or they had yet to do anything other than talk about being heroes.

"Scarlet and I were having a private conversation."

Eclipse leaned on my bar, barely glancing at me. "You wouldn't know what to do with a lady like this." I couldn't argue the point, but I'd be more than happy to show him why safe words were a necessity.

"A rum and coke."

"We're out of rum." I didn't need to turn around to know there were a dozen bottles on the shelf. It was petty. A better bartender would have pulled from the well and charged him for the top-shelf. I didn't like his tone. Hell, I didn't like the man's face.

"Excuse me?"

"I can piss in a bottle and call it lemonade." It was over the line. If Scarlet hadn't been ready to retire, she'd have sent me home without my tips. Thankfully, she couldn't use her powers with her jaw gaping at the insult.

"You'll be the first thing to go when I buy the club."

"The day you buy it is the day I resign. No respectable hero is coming to a club with a poseur for a host. They'd rather be at the donut shop with the police."

"You petulant—"

"Stop a couple of Norse Gods from waging war downtown and then we can talk. After you take your clothes to the cleaners, of course."

Nobody knew Eclipse's powers. By the name, I suspected it had something to do with the moon. Or perhaps he spoke to some lunar God who imbued him with strength. He wouldn't dare show up to the Alley as a lowly human. Though, if anybody was going to do it, it'd be him.

The hero's teeth clenched. I had half a mind to crack a beer bottle over the cooler and then jab him in the neck. I didn't want to stab him, not really, but if it made him get his hands dirty, it might be worth the attempted murder charge. Though, the more I thought about it, sinking the bottle—

"Both of you, stop."

I looked down at the bottle in my hand. Had I grabbed it? I didn't like Eclipse. The thought of him buying the club left me filled with more than a little hate. I was a lover, not a fighter. I was more likely to get Eclipse in bed and mock the size of his penis before causing him harm.

Scarlet's words rippled through my body and I held my tongue as I set the bottle down. Even Eclipse found himself trapped by her abilities. There were few who could resist her siren's call. The anger vanished almost as quickly as it appeared.

"I'm sorry," she mouthed before taking Eclipse by the arm. "Follow me," she said, forcing him to leave the bar. As she guided the man through his band of cronies, they turned, following their cult leader. I didn't like any of them, but as I stared at the bottle, I needed to take inventory of my anger.

"Alejandro, what's going on with you?" I whispered.

"What do you think they're talking about?"

Bruno had abandoned his post at the door shortly after one. It was rare for a hero to show up that late unless they had been in a brawl. Instead of pretending he was the gatekeeper for the club, he turned to speculate about Eclipse and Scarlet's arrangement.

"I can't believe he's going to be our boss," I hissed.

"My boss, you mean. He's going to fire your ass soon as the ink dries."

He hushed as Verdant approached the bar. For an alien, he appeared almost human. It took a thorough inspection to see his arms were a little longer, his chest wider, and eyes further apart. Oh, and he hovered somewhere north of seven feet. He had been a regular at the Alley for as long as I had been slinging drinks. When your planet blows up and you get stuck on Earth, might as well go to a place that serves a solid cocktail.

"Little man," he said with a hearty laugh. Bruno let out a snort at the moniker.

"Hello, fat man," Verdant added. I snorted. Years on the planet and he hadn't properly socialized. It made for amusing conversations. It took getting used to, but he was about as honest as they came. I always wondered if the *rest* of him was as long and girthy. Based on the bulge in his emerald green pants, I had my suspicions.

"Ple'nian ale, little man. I thank you now."

I slapped a napkin on the table and turned around to the shelves of alcohol. It had taken Scarlet months to track down a bootlegger that specialized in intergalactic alcohol. But with her connections, she had the delicacy recreated. We always had a bottle on hand just for Verdant. Her ability to go above and beyond was legendary, a legacy I doubted Eclipse would uphold.

I grabbed the decanter and turned around just in time to see a small portal open and a hand snatch the napkin before vanishing. I couldn't imagine what Theo was up to, or why he didn't show up to talk while having a drink on the house. There were quirks about heroes, and at some point, I stopped asking questions.

Placing down another napkin, I poured a glass. Verdant greedily chugged until nothing remained. He pushed the glass back in my direction. The hero didn't have to ask as I filled it a second time. He slapped money on the table.

"Little man, keep the remaining sum of currency."

"Thanks, big man."

"Fat man, be well." He gave Bruno a nudge with his elbow before returning to a group of alien supers.

I replaced the bottle and came back to see a napkin sitting on the counter. With a raise of the eyebrow, I couldn't figure out what Theo was doing. The napkin had scribbles on it. Was he trying to be cute? Was he playing a game? I had questions, and a note on a napkin wasn't going to—

"Oh," I said.

"Oh? What? Is there another power demonstration happening?" Bruno turned around, scanning the room. He'd act tough and tell them to keep the show to a minimum, but there wasn't much he could do if it turned into a pissing contest.

I eyed the note again. *Down for a quickie?*

I gave a very deliberate nod. Theo could have a portal anywhere in the room where he watched. I placed another napkin down on the counter, hoping to see his hand snatch it away before returning with directions. I took inventory of all the places at the Alley I had gotten it on with superheroes. The bathroom? The back alley? The parking lot? The roof? The top of the piano?

¡Joder! I had a lot of sex in this building.

I watched the napkin, the Alley's logo dead center, but the portal never opened. There was always the chance he got called away, or he discovered the parking lot wasn't as private as one would expect. It wouldn't be the only opportunity, so I tried not to dwell on it.

Bruno returned to the bar, deflated that nothing exploded in the bar. "Is it just me, or has business died off more than usual? Things were looking up after the depowering,"

"I bet it's..."

My train of thought derailed as a mysterious force tugged at the zipper of my slacks. I froze. There was no way my face remained neutral. I had to concentrate so my eyes wouldn't go wide. The zipper reached the bottom, and there was a pause. I didn't dare look down and bring attention to what was happening underneath the bar.

"Yes?" Bruno asked.

"Oh." Focus. I could carry on a conversation while airing my junk. "They probably heard Eclipse is buying the bar. Who would want to come..." A hand reached into the zipper, tugging at the fabric of my briefs. "...here when he's going to own it."

See, being fondled didn't slow my gift for gab.

"I suppose," he said. "You're as good as fired. Did I tell you I got approached for a job?"

The cool air hit my skin as Theo exposed my cock and balls through the fly of my pants. I had to do a quick inspection to make sure none of the other bartenders had stayed after being relieved for the night. Never had I been more thrilled to be the only man working.

"You don't say?"

I stole a quick glance. I should have seen an erect penis reaching for the heavens. Instead, my groin pressed against an invisible barrier and my cock was missing. In any other situation, it'd have sent a man into a frenzy. One of the few joys in life was knowing our little buddy was always there to help get us into trouble. After the last encounter with Theo, I knew my cock and balls were somewhere else in the universe, being admired by that sexy bear.

"Yeah, the head of security at Revelations approached me. He said someone had dropped my name in a conversation. Asked if I'd be willing to come in and have an interview."

As fingers gently grazed the smoothness of my balls, I struggled to pay attention to Bruno. Revelations. Job. "Wait, what? That trash magazine wants to hire you?" His tongue replaced his fingers, the warmth of his breath moving from one testicle to the other. I'd have called this torture. Listening to Bruno talk about job opportunities was taking away from the excitement of Theo servicing me from somewhere else in the world.

"Apparently, the big guy over there has been getting some threats. I can't imagine why. It's a magazine about superheroes. If he's making the heroes angry, then what does he think I'm going to do?"

The tongue ran along the bottom of my cock until it reached the tip. I did my best to hide the shiver as he nibbled on my foreskin, taking quick licks at the head. Sex in public had always been arousing. The thrill of getting caught was as hot as mounting a hero in the stairwell. But never in a million years did I think I'd be making eye contact with Bruno while getting my knob polished.

"I know—" Theo swallowed my cock. I coughed to hide the gasp. "Pee-ple from there. It's shady." Theo wasn't quick with his mouth. He'd sink to the base, pause, then back off until he nearly let my cock slip from his lips. I leaned forward, resting my elbows on the bar, pushing my hips as far forward as the portal allowed.

"Shady, I can handle—if they have good health insurance. I just need something where I can put money away. I'm old enough to know I don't want to be working until I die. When the time comes, I'd like to put Sophie through college."

I tried to make it look as if I were rocking my ass back and forth, but it was all I could do to not hump the air. Theo's consistent and steady rhythm tried to drag out the experience. Thinking about coming in front of a room full of heroes, that image had my libido rushing toward the imaginary finish line.

"You can do better." I nearly grunted as Theo wrapped his fingers around my balls. His tempo quickened. He was being greedy and wanted me to come.

"I think Scarlet spoiled us."

"Yeah." The tingling settled in. I wanted the experience to last, but my cock had other plans.

"I don't know. Maybe I'm just panicking. Who knows, working for Eclipse might not be so bad."

"It'll be bad, so bad." I almost dropped my face to the counter as the warmth washed over my body. The amount of suction created by Theo made it clear that he was urging me on, wanting me to fill his mouth as I came.

"There is something off about him." I wanted to agree, but right now, I needed to focus on not growling as an orgasm tore through my body. "Have you noticed his henchmen hover around him like groupies?" Yup. Busy, Bruno. "Or that he's always clean?" Stop talking. "I can't put my finger on it yet, but there's something odd."

Leo, the Leopard King, sauntered up to the counter. "Martini, dirty."

I grabbed a beer out of the cooler and slammed it down

on the counter. With a twist of the top, I pushed it in his direction. "Out of Martinis."

"It's just—"

"Beer. On the house."

"But—"

"No."

"Can you—"

"You're about to get warm water."

I locked eyes with the man as the orgasm rippled through my body. The only thing more persuasive than free beer is the cold eyes of a man trying to come. He snatched it and walked away as I shot through a portal to parts unknown.

"Are you okay?"

My legs threatened to cave, forcing me to lean over the bar again. Theo took pity, holding still as he swallowed. He waited a minute before carefully tucking my sensitive cock into my pants and lifting the zipper. Without a word, the portal vanished, and he left me trying to remember the events of the last ten minutes.

"Wait, did you say something?" Bruno's face went slack as he blinked rapidly. By his expression, that was the wrong question to ask.

The grin on my face would have made the most notorious villain proud. "Sorry, my mind was elsewhere."

14

———

OTHER THAN ECLIPSE GIVING ME A CONDESCENDING WAVE AS he left, the rest of the night had been uneventful. I hoped to bump into Theo and be able to chat while on the clock. Well, what I really wanted was to spend the evening riding him until I hit my calorie goal. After the stunt he pulled tonight, the least I could do was leave him exhausted in the bedroom.

I stood outside Midnight Alley, waving as Bruno drove by on his motorcycle. He knew me well enough to not offer a ride. More often than not, I'd get a ride in a pimped-out sports car or invisible jet as I rode away with the flavor of the night. It did leave me wondering if my night would end with my clothes on the floor.

A: You up?

The triple dot of an impending reply blinked, then

stopped. I scowled at the phone. Nobody liked seeing the dots, only to be silenced. I could excuse a lot when dealing with superheroes. But being ghosted—

"Figured this was easier."

I nearly squealed as I jumped. When distance wasn't a factor, it was shocking where somebody might appear. "Okay, new rule. No more teleporting from behind."

"I mean," he laughed, "that was my next trick."

Dammit. I wanted to be mad, but my penis apparently liked the suggestion. I turned around to find myself looking at Theo and not his superpowered alter ego. While I thought the leather suit and mask were sexy, nothing compared to the smile that stretched from his face into his eyes. He was so much sexier as a bearish citizen.

"How's Stonewall?"

He smiled at the mention of his husband. It was still weird to ask the man I texted all hours of the night about his partner, but it'd be foolish to act as if he didn't exist. And while I was still sorting through my baggage, I genuinely liked the bruiser.

"Really good. He's with a team helping the Magus fight a demon? A god? What do you call the person who rules a layer of Hell?"

"Can't say I've been asked that before."

"I might get a call from him to evac. Just in case I have to dash off." He took my hand, running his thumb over my knuckles. "Still weird, isn't it?"

"A little."

He raised my hand, kissing it. "I appreciate the effort."

"Want to walk back to my place?" Stupid question asking a man who could bend space-time. "I've been on my feet all night, and I desperately need to put them up."

Two portals opened on either side of him. I seem to remember a similar trick. He definitely knew how to bring the wow factor to a casual evening.

"There's no way you can beat sunrise in Paris. Where does this one lead?"

"Do you trust me?"

Through one portal, I could see my couch, my incredibly soft and comfortable couch. I could almost hear it calling my name, summoning me to sit down and let it hold me in a warm hug. I couldn't make out the destination on the other. It could have been anywhere on the planet. If I were alone, I'd have opted for my living room, but with the boyish smile on his face, eager to show me another exotic location, I couldn't resist.

"I trust you." I meant it.

"Quick warning. Portals going this far can make you a little dizzy."

Before I could ask questions, he pulled me through. We were on the other side in an instant, but my insides took a second to catch up. I staggered and Theo caught me, holding me tight as I fought my way through the nausea.

"Dios mío." With a deep breath, the world solidified under my feet. "Where did you take us? Australia?"

"A little further."

"Where on Earth…"

We were standing in a grassy field, except what should have been a lush green blanket on the ground was a vibrant purple. Even the sky held a tinge of purple and magenta. Wherever we were, it was night. There were hills in the distance, just short of being mountains. There were no animals, no real sounds other than a gentle breeze.

I gasped as a series of streaks appeared high above, speeding through the veil of darkness. Dozens more followed as a meteor storm filled the sky. As I followed their path, I barely had words to describe it. Hanging in the sky was a vast, amorphous blob of colors. Somewhere out in space, I was watching a celestial event unfold.

"This isn't Earth," I whispered.

"This isn't even the Milky Way."

"What is it?"

"You're watching a star be born."

"A sun?"

"The planet has two," he explained. "Someday, it'll have a third."

"So much better than Paris," I mumbled.

It was one thing to see my sun from a new location. High above Paris had been stunning. While the city felt claustrophobic, wherever he had brought me felt as if it were... I couldn't wrap my head around it. It *was* a different world.

"Theo," I turned back to him. While I had been taking in the sky, he had been watching me. "It's beautiful." I kissed the man. As I held the sides of his face, it came with the realization that I had kissed a superhero on a distant planet underneath an event that almost no human on Earth would ever witness. Cinnamon and shooting stars.

"You're going to need to up your game for our next date."

There was a pause to his usual quip. "So there's going to be a next date?" The bravado slipped from his voice. I studied his face and could see the vulnerability creeping in as he broke eye contact. Heroes could save the world without hesitation, but for something as simple as a date, they carried the same insecurities as the rest of us.

I took his hand and spun myself, so it was draped over my shoulders. Pulling him tight, I assured him this wouldn't be our last date. "I'm pretty sure there's another date in our future. Why would you think otherwise?"

"It's not exactly a conventional situation."

"You mean the flashy leather outfits? That's more common in my life than you'd think."

"You know what I mean."

I did. I still hadn't processed that the guy I was into had a husband that he loved. Every time I thought about it, I could hear outside expectations of what "should be" piling on my shoulders. How would I explain it to the guys at lunch? Would they consider me the other man? Was this an attempt for Theo and Stonewall to fix a failing relationship?

"I do. Is it bad I'm trying not to think about it? It feels like the world is telling me to do one thing and…" I kissed his hand. "I'm not so sure I agree with that mindset anymore. I like you enough to reevaluate."

"Whoa now. I'm going to get turned on."

I snorted. Okay, we returned to our normal scheduled program. A snarky bartender and dashing superhero sitting underneath the birth of a new star. There were worse ways to spend the evening.

"El memo," I cursed with a laugh.

"Ouch, you wound me."

His body tensed and he dropped his arm as he stared off into the distance. Something happened that I couldn't make out. Was there danger? Did he sense something in the universe?

"Bluetooth," he pointed to his ear. "Stonewall needs an evac."

"Should we go back?"

"I'll be right back. Don't move."

The portal opened, and on the other side a massive dragon roared as it breathed fire, only stopped by a man conjuring magical barriers. Before I could speak, Theo transformed into EO, his clothes vanishing, replaced by his suit, and he jumped through the portal. Once it closed, I was left on an alien planet somewhere far outside the familiar boundaries of the Ward. Hell, far outside my familiar Milky Way.

"I wonder how much an Uber would cost?"

15

THIRTY MINUTES HAD PASSED SINCE EO HAD DASHED OFF TO save the day. Butterflies had transformed into angry bats in my stomach. What started as a worry that someone injured him quickly turned toward my own situation. It did not surprise me to find zero bars on my cell. I had poor reception in my apartment, and being light-years from home wouldn't make it any better.

There was nothing that gave any indication of civilization on the planet. I knew there were plenty of worlds with life across the cosmos. For some reason, their citizens always chose Earth to defend and protect. The more I thought about it, I'd need to ask Bernard why they chose Earth.

"Hello?" When nobody responded, I plonked myself onto the grass. Running my hands along the ground, I decided I might as well settle in. There were worse places to be stranded. "He could have left me somewhere with a beach. We'll have to make that a prerequisite for the future."

Lying back, the star forming above the planet was more majestic than anything I had ever seen. I snapped a photo with my phone for proof. It defied any word I could find in my vocabulary. Beautiful? Stunning? Breathtaking? None of them did it justice. I'd have to talk to Griffin to see if his art background had words for this creation. It was the birth of something primal. I might as well sit back and enjoy it.

A flock of flying creatures passed overhead, the first sign of life on the alien planet. Three of them danced back and forth, touching a layer of the sky that created streaks of fire in their wake. Were they phoenixes? Is this where the myth originated? We had established that aliens put the pyramids on Earth. Maybe other civilizations were the same?

"Hell. No air conditioning. Hostile creatures. Zero stars. Do not recommend."

I rolled over to see EO kneeling on the ground, steam rising off his body. Stonewall stepped out of the portal, patting down tiny flames scattered across his suit. "I want to speak with the manager."

They were a comedy act. "Are you guys okay?"

"A minor demon, they said. It'll be easy, they said. We'll be done with it in no time, they said. What I learned—

mages lie. Those magic wielders forgot to mention the demon ruled a pocket dimension."

Stonewall raised a middle finger behind him to where the portal had been. "You're not getting a Christmas card this year!"

"We'll be fine," EO said. He patted a spot on his chest and his clothes morphed from his suit to street clothes. I'd have to ask him about getting something like that for work.

"Wait, this isn't Earth," Stonewall said. "Hon, where did you bring us?"

Well, this was about to get awkward.

"Brought Alejandro to see the Whisper Galaxy."

Stonewall spun about, taking inventory of his surroundings. It didn't seem to bother him that they weren't on Earth. I had to wonder if this was common for heroes. Did Theo bring everybody to the far reaches of the universe?

"Huh," he said. "You never bring me to distant galaxies."

"You complain about the lack of Wi-Fi."

"No Wi-Fi?" He gasped. "Send me back to Hell."

I couldn't help but laugh. I was starting to understand how I fit into this equation. If Stonewall didn't like these field trips, why shouldn't Theo go on them with another person? Stonewall's words from the other night finally made sense.

I put a finger to my lips and made a hushing noise.

Rolling over, I pointed up at the flying creatures. They looked almost like manta rays swimming across the sky. As they bobbed up and down, streaks of fire followed, and as they wove about one another, it made a beautiful and elegant pattern.

"Wow," Stonewall said. He finished patting out the fire and took a seat on the other side of Theo. I had to admit I was being hyper vigilant in their mannerisms. Even with his suit on, the moment he sat down and rested a hand on Theo's knee, I could see the man behind the mask emerge.

Before the insecurities of being the third wheel could set in, Theo rested a hand on my shoulder, rubbing it slowly. This dynamic would take more explaining than any of my one-night stands. But as we admired the scenery, something about it felt right. Simple. Tender. I thought I could get used to this.

"Careful, Alejandro. He lures you in with romantic dates to faraway places and before you know it, he's leaving dishes in the sink."

"Oh, hells no. You're going to be scrubbing those before bedtime."

"Good luck," he added. "I've been trying for years."

"I could leave you both here."

"Should we discuss the trail of laundry?" Julian continued.

"You know, leave you both... in another galaxy." Theo's threats weren't deterring.

"What other bad habits should I be aware of?"

"That's it. I'm going back to Hell."

"Blanket hog," Julian laughed.

"It took one sleepover for me to learn that one."

"This isn't fun anymore!" Theo cried out before hiding his face in his hands. He could protest all he wanted. There was no hiding the grin on his face. He might be a bear of a man, but he was giddy having his husband and... whatever I was, teasing him.

Julian reached across Theo, patting me on the stomach. "We'll start a support group. It'll be in a pillow fort and all the blankets you can ask for. I'll bring wine."

"I'm seeing a divorce lawyer tomorrow."

"Husband, he'd side with me in a heartbeat."

I was about to pile on more teasing when a comet passed overhead. It was close enough to see the atmosphere wrap around the front, leaving a long tail of white behind it. I had seen shooting stars before, somewhere off in distant worlds, but not like this. The boulder burned away until there was nothing left.

Just as I was about to speak, three more appeared. Somewhere in the cosmos, we were getting a show that no other humans could witness. The sky sparkled as dozens more followed. I turned to see their faces filled with a sense of childlike awe.

Theo caught me staring, but I couldn't look away. His hand found mine, squeezing it tightly as we spent the next hour making wishes as we watched hundreds of meteors. I had fought against thinking of him as more than a fling, fearful that it'd be complicated. My face turned red, a blush as his eyes held the same sense of wonder as they had watching the sky.

I processed, and I liked the conclusions I discovered.

16

———————

"A country bar? I didn't even know these existed in Vanguard."

I patted Theo on the cheek. "Stick with me, handsome, and I'll show you all the fun night spots."

"I'm seeing that."

The Stallion was a good ol' fashioned country bar. On one side of the room, walled off by a waist-high wall, were tables and the bar. The rustic charm came from the rough wood, horns hanging on the wall, and coarse rope used to line the tables. It wasn't my usual hang-out spot, but when Theo said he wanted to try something different, it immediately came to mind. Sure, it wasn't the Eiffel Tower, but I was willing to bet it was something he had never seen.

"Shots. Tequila. No, make that two doubles."

"A double?" Theo's eyes went wide.

The bartender gave Theo the once over. "Sure the city slicker can handle it?" I had to admit, I nearly laughed out loud at Theo's decorative button-down shirt, complete with bolo tie. As I saw the boots, I couldn't contain myself. Before we left, I gave him an hour to get ready. I thought he had gone into his bedroom to change, but now I was certain he teleported to Texas.

"What?" he asked.

"Nothing. Just admiring how adorable you look." I shook my head, laughing. With a quick double tap on the bar, Luke prepared to wow Theo.

"Double it is," he said, adding a whistle for effect.

The Stallion was known for many things, but above all else, it was known for a good time. Luke reached up to the cowboy hat, giving a slight nod before he snatched a bottle off the shelf. He couldn't offer a simple pour. He tossed the bottle, letting it spin as he reached behind his back, catching it with a practiced hand. I should know. I taught him the trick.

"You still tending at the hero club?" he asked.

"Until they fire me."

"Until they fire him."

I laughed at our echo. Good to know we were thinking the same thing.

"Al, sounds like the gentleman knows you plenty well enough."

Luke pushed two glasses filled to the brim across the

bar. The rim had been salted, and a napkin held a slice of lime. In my younger days, this would have been the start of my evening. The fastest way to get tips from patrons was to drink alongside them. It might explain why my youth was hazy.

Luke moved on to his next client. I handed Theo the glass. He didn't look quite convinced. If he couldn't handle a double shot of tequila, he might have to reconsider who he dated.

He went for the shot when I stopped him. Shaking my head, I laughed. "We have to toast. Can't take your first shot of the night without it. So, what do we drink to?"

"Health? A night without supervillains?"

"Si te lleva el diablo, que te lleve en buen caballo."

"I understood diablo."

"Mi madre used to say it. It means to take risks, even when they're big."

"To taking a risk." He lifted his glass.

I licked the salt on the rim, slammed the shot, and bit down on the lime. Theo sipped his, choking down the clear liquid. My cowboy grimaced as he swiped the lime, trying to chase away the burn. With his teeth clamped down, the green of the rind replacing his smile, I couldn't ignore his charm. His beard begged to be grabbed and pulled in for a kiss so I could taste the booze on his lips. I could see Theo being dangerous in all the right ways.

"I didn't take you for a cowboy," he said.

I held up two fingers for Luke and pointed to some beer. "Cowboy? Where do you think those hombres' got their sense of style? Don't get me started on the food."

I took the beers from Luke and headed to a table. The band had started their sound check, and I could see my plan for the evening laid out before me. I was going to see if my hero could brave more than villains.

"I don't know what I expected..." He watched a group of locals clanking beer bottles. "But this isn't it. You continue to surprise me."

"Says the man who can..."

"Nope." His hand shot up, covering my mouth. "Tonight is nothing but normal. I'm just a man, a poorly dressed man apparently, on a date with a stallion."

I shook my head, scrunching up my nose. "We need to work on that label."

"Stud?"

"They *are* used for breeding."

He shot me a wink. "We'll see if you get that lucky, Mr. Martinez."

"You haven't told me what this poorly dressed man does for work."

"Insurance adjuster."

My jaw dropped. By night, he teleported about the city, saving people from evil. He could bench press me without straining. This hero had a desk job? Something about that just seemed off.

"We can't all have flashy jobs to pay the bills," he smirked. "I oversee the city's claims department. With so many superheroes, you'd be surprised how often somebody calls because their car was thrashed by a super confrontation."

"So you..." I snorted. Theo's nighttime persona caused the damage, and his day job recovered the costs. "Well, damn. If that's not job security, I don't know what is."

"My turn." His brow furrowed, making him cuter. I don't know how it was possible, but he had the perfect blend of boyish charm and sex appeal. I couldn't wait to show him off to the guys. The thought happened before I could process it. I had never introduced Griffin or Xander to the men I hung out with. Even Bernard only met Dan once just before... nope. I wasn't thinking about that tonight.

"Siblings?"

"Nope."

"Parents?"

"Mi madre lives in Arizona. My dad is somewhere in Mexico, I think. We're not close."

"Why Vanguard?"

Good question and the answer bordered on comical. "I couldn't stay in Mexico. I wanted to see the world. So I applied to Vanguard University. It became home. I couldn't imagine living anywhere else. It's a weird city. Distrito Federal has a few superheroes, but not like Vanguard. This is the only place where you can have a city invasion by breakfast and see goblins raiding the streets by dinner. I wanted excitement, and I found it here."

The band started as we bounced from one topic to the next. As this side of the bar slowly emptied onto the dance floor, we talked about our upbringings, learning to drive, and our inability to keep plants alive. With each word out of his mouth, I found myself captivated. For a superhero, he had no idea that I had lured him into a trap.

"I don't know how to say this, but you are the worst dancer," I confessed. "I mean, the other night, it bordered on painful."

His confidence brushed off the insult. "You didn't seem to mind."

"Of course not. Have you seen yourself? I'd let you read stereo instructions, and it'd still put me in the mood."

"So..."

He let the statement hang in the air. I turned to the crowd line dancing. Nearly two-dozen people finished spinning about, fingers hooked in their belts as they tapped their heels to the music. I turned back, deliberate, slow, giving him time to sort out the smile stretching from ear to ear.

"What? Out there? No way."

"If the boot fits." If I smiled any harder, it'd become permanent. "You can stop a snake woman, but a little line dancing scares you? And here I thought you were brave."

I took a swig and walked toward the dance floor. The lead singer of the band started strumming when I looked over my shoulder to see Theo downing his beer in a rush. He stood, adjusting his bolo, and followed me onto the dance floor.

"I hate you right now," he said.

"Let's teach you some dance moves, and then I'll show you a few more later."

I took his hand, placing him in one line next to an older gentleman. "It's his first time," I warned his neighbor.

The man gave Theo a once over. "I couldn't tell." He smiled, revealing a silver tooth. "I'll take good care of him."

By the time I reached the line opposite him, the older man was instructing him. Theo tried to keep up, but it was obvious that without his portals, he lacked coordination. While he might not make the best dance partner, the determination on his face made it even more endearing. Powers or not, Theo had my attention.

The music started. Men bowed, tipping hats as the women dipped in a curtsey. As the line moved, the older man kept his hand on Theo's back to guide him. He might not have the footwork down, but at least he could spin to avoid causing a pile-up.

As the two lines converged, we were inches apart. I stole a kiss as I grabbed his hand, our palms pressed together. He missed the toe, heel and if it hadn't been for my finger hooked on his belt loop, he'd have stepped in the wrong direction.

"I'm the world's worst dancer," he laughed.

I'd have agreed at the start. But by the third round of dancing, he had started keeping up. There might be hope for his strip teases. The music ended and the older gentleman stepped up behind Theo.

"We'll make a country boy out of you yet."

"I don't know about that," Theo confessed.

"Same time next week?"

I raised an eyebrow at Theo. Chad would be delighted to know I remembered his rule book. You never ended a date before scheduling the next date. Rule #7, I think?

"What do you say? Next week?"

I'm pretty sure Theo bit back a smile. "It's a date."

"We'll be here," I told the man.

"Does this deserve a yeehaw?" asked Theo.

"Is he serious?"

"City boys, am I right" I laughed. The older man patted us both on the shoulder before leaving.

"So I shouldn't ask about bull riding later?"

We might have a second date, but it appeared this one was far from over.

17

———

The portal transported me from my living room to the HideOut. It might be abusing Theo's abilities, but I couldn't help but make an entrance and show off for the guys. Every day they rolled their eyes at my stories, convinced I over-exaggerated my evening trysts. But as I stepped through, hands on my hips, I coughed, clearing my throat.

"Wait! Where'd you—"

I waved my hand at Griffin, silencing him. "Perks of dating a teleporter." The moment I said it, Bernard's furry lip turned upward. I'd have to thank him for his sagely advice when we had a quiet moment. Right now, I wanted to show off for these goons.

Another portal opened up to my side and EO's upper body leaned out. "Remember the teasing last night?" he whispered the words. In the next sentence, however, he made sure everybody in the coffee shop heard him. "Have a great day at school, kiddo." He kissed me on the cheek and vanished.

"I will have my revenge," I grumbled.

"Well, he's cute." Our resident matchmaker turned barista already had my coffee in hand. He thrust the cup in my direction while his free hand felt around the air, looking for the portal. "Does he have a brother? A dad? I'd let him call me daddy."

Well, this entrance had gone sideways quickly. "Go call your husband and take a cold shower."

"Admiring is not touching. I have permission to gawk."

"He is cute," Xander added. "I'd let him call me daddy."

"He could call me whatever he wanted," Griffin said.

We all turned to Bernard, waiting for him to add the last zinger before we moved on to our usual morning ritual. As he sipped his coffee, he watched each of us. With a guffaw, he set it down. "He's not calling anybody daddy."

"Really? That's it?" Xander said. "You're losing your—"

"Papi, on the other hand..."

The burly man shot me a smile. Nobody dared call Bernard a daddy bear except me. It's how I convinced myself I was his favorite. Either that or I had worn him to where he gave up hope of us having a normal relationship. I thought about that furry puppy pile in my bed.

"I know that look," Xander started.

"Yup. He's having sex thoughts," Griffin finished. "We could be here a while."

"I'm going to put in a double order of eggs and sausage. I have a feeling you've been burning the calories." Chad's elbow to my side jostled me back to reality. How did this coffee wind up in my hand?

"Should we just let him tell us about the freaky sex now and get it out of the way?" I shot Xander a dirty look. Over his shoulder, I could see the counter and the orange thermos meant for the Zipper. The colors reminded me of the sky the night before. Even millions of miles away on our boring Earth, it was a memory I'd never forget.

I took a sip of coffee before blowing on the liquid. "Jóvenes, I watched a star be born last night."

"Wait, in the bedroom?" asked Griffin.

"Get your mind out of the gutter. He took us to a planet far away from here. There were meteors, a nebula thing creating a new star, and these birds that lit up the sky like fire."

"Did you just say you were on another planet?" asked Xander.

"Who is this 'us' you speak of?" asked Griffin.

"EO and his husband Stonewall. It was date night for EO and me, and then he had to go save his husband from a god in Hell. We spent most of the night watching the stars."

"You're dating a guy with a husband? Wait, did you say

a god?" Griffin's eyebrow raised. I suspected people would have questions about that.

"I don't care who he's dating. You can't be running off to other galaxies. What if something happened?" Xander had a point. But after watching EO's heroics, I knew I was in safe hands.

"Bernard?" Griffin threw a sugar packet at the man.

"I'm still processing the fact Alejandro told *us* to get *our* minds out of the gutter."

"I say this with love." Xander reached across the table, resting a hand on mine. "Do you really want to get invested with a guy you can't have?"

"Back it up, Mr. Monogamous. Just because his relationship isn't seen in every rom-com movie doesn't mean it isn't valid. The stupid smile on his face says everything we need to know."

I appreciated Xander's concern. It came from a place of love. But it was Bernard's words that made my heart sing. I could almost overlook the caterpillar above his lip and kiss the man. Now that we had gotten his secret identity out into the open, I could imagine him or his caped alter ego getting naked.

"Sorry," Xander said. "I didn't mean anything—"

"I know." Truthfully, I did. Xander would crack the skull of any person who did wrong by his friends. "I'm going into this with my eyes open. Right now, I'm just enjoying the experience."

"Does this mean no more regaling us with your sexcapades?" asked Griffin.

"Ha! EO can teleport. Have you ever given yourself a blow job? Nope, don't even dare lie about it. Dating a teleporter has some serious perks in the bedroom."

"That's the Alejandro we love," Xander said, raising his coffee into the air. "May sex with your boyfriend stay freaky until the end of time."

Boyfriend. It hadn't been since Dan left I considered the word part of my vocabulary. The perk of a one-night stand was that they were both free of a relationship and, by design, remained a single night. I didn't want to think about how this panned out in a week or a month. I could barely manage thinking about it right now. If I thought about the future, I'd likely call the whole thing off and hide.

"So tell us..." Griffin's words trailed off as he reached for his phone. It had become a common occurrence. We could barely make it through breakfast before our phones sounded with the HeroApp™ alerts. I thought the supervillains of Vanguard City knew when I was trying to eat my breakfast.

The vibration in my pocket intensified, a sign that something was about to go horribly wrong. Bernard remained the only person at the table who refused to check his phone. I assumed nothing that dangerous for the three of us really applied to him. Or maybe he waited for the

Centurions to call him on his secret phone before he sprung into duty.

"Not curious?" How else could I ask a superhero why he wasn't springing into action?

"I'll be curious once I finish my coffee."

If I could wield the fury of Mother Nature, I'd probably finish getting a caffeine injection. Red alert? Great, was Ludo the living volcano threatening to destroy the planet again? Big men didn't handle the heat well. If we were rooting for global climate change, I'd always side with Lord Frost and his snow giants.

"Those five goons again?" Griffin groaned.

My back stiffened at the words. There were a thousand supervillains capable of kidnapping any of us. But only one had reached into my soul and manifested my darkest fears. Sure, the man in white could probably punch a hole through my chest, but even now, the terrors inched their way into my peripheral.

"Not worth…"

"He nearly killed me." I don't know why I hadn't told Bernard about it. Perhaps I was ashamed of the thoughts the villain forced me to confront. But I couldn't let the table dismiss somebody capable of driving a person to kill themselves on a subway track.

"Al…" Bernard's paw covered my hand. "Anything we can do?"

I shook my head. "Just be careful out there." I stared at

Xander as I spoke, but the words were meant for Bernard as well. If the man in white had brought my insecurities to the surface and weaponized them, who knew what he could do to these two?

Before either responded, the coffee shop filled with alarms. I checked the screen, and the HeroApp™ flashed a proximity alert. Somewhere nearby, the villains were roaming about, and now we'd need to decide if the HideOut was safe enough to treat as our bunker while we waited for heroes to save the day.

"They're down the street," Griffin said.

Both Bernard and Xander got to their feet as the patrons grabbed their to-go cups and fled through the entrance. Nobody wanted to be trapped in the coffee shop if the villains ramped up their property damage.

"Bernard," Xander jumped to his feet, "you stay with them. I'm going to get to the ambulance."

"Me?" Bernard raised an eyebrow. "You keep an eye on them. The Centurions..."

They continued to argue about which should stay and protect Griffin and me, as if we were incapable of saving ourselves. Now I understood why women were angry about being labeled as damsels in distress. Hopefully, Xander backed down so Bernard could slip into his spandex and save the day. At any moment, they were about to slap one another.

Or they would have, except for the explosion.

18

"Mister, are you okay?"

The tiny voice barely broke through the ringing in my ears. I didn't open my eyes as my stomach attempted to twist itself into knots. Any more sensory input and I'd hurl my breakfast down the front of my shirt.

We had fled, maybe? My brain struggled to recall the last few minutes. Chad pushed us out the back of the cafe while the Nocturnals slugged it out with heroes. An explosion. Yes, the windows had exploded as the fight grew close. I ran out the back, and then... I hurt, an ache that reached into the core of my bones.

"Is he even alive?"

Two tiny voices. They weren't screaming. I'd take that as a good sign. It took a minute. Si. Chad ushered everybody out the back before the fight could find its way inside. Everything was hazy. I probably had a concussion.

"I think he's dead." The tiny voices were like waking up to a siren after a night of cheap booze. Children. I remembered. They were trapped in the alley. Everybody was running for safety when I spotted them running into a derelict building. Did I honestly run into a collapsing building to save children? I don't even like children.

A finger poked my cheek.

I *really* don't like children.

"He's alive," said a young boy. He was anywhere from six to sixteen. Like I said, I'm not a fan of anybody too young to drink.

"Stop touching me," I mumbled. I opened my eyes to narrow slits. The room didn't spin any faster than before. I expected light to burn into my cornea, but wherever we were, it was almost pitch dark. I had grabbed them and ran into a freezer, but the details remained fuzzy.

"He's mean." The level of annoyance in her voice shouldn't have been possible at that age. Nope, no thanks. No appreciation for nearly dying. I joked I liked men to ensure I never found out of accidental offspring. Instead of being thankful, I was mean.

"You two okay?" I coughed, as the dust in the air worked its way down my throat.

"I think so," said the boy.

"Me too," replied his companion. "We saved you, mister."

"I'm pretty sure I did the saving." I think? Between the adrenaline and explosions, there was a good chance I was dead. These two little misfits could be a personification of Heaven and Hell waging a war for my soul. I nearly laughed at the idea of getting into Heaven.

"Nuh-uh. We dragged you to safety. You almost got crushed by the wall." She was mighty proud at the fact she had saved a grown-up. Perhaps she was the next generation of hero. Perhaps kids weren't so bad after all.

"Crushed. Like the dead kind of crushed."

I take it back. I still disliked the ankle biters. But she shone a flashlight toward an enormous chunk of cement, and I could see the lines in the dust. The disturbance led right to where a slab of concrete had landed on the floor. The little bastardos *had* saved me. I couldn't let them see my appreciation. Kids are like sharks, a bit of affection, and they circle for the kill.

"How long was I out?"

"All the loud noises stopped."

The girl maintained a stiff upper lip despite the fact we were buried under a pile of rubble. The boy, however, every time her light flickered and left us in the dark, tensed. Like all the citizens of Vanguard, we were closer to annihilation than we wanted to admit. Unlike the adults, these kids didn't have a say in where they lived.

"I'm going to get us out of here." I wasn't sure how, but I didn't need to share that.

"Do you have super strength?" The girl's question had an edge of disbelief. I'd be recommending to her parents they put her up for adoption. But before I could break the news they were raising a snot, I needed to find an opening in the rubble big enough for us to squeeze through.

I tried sitting up but found the space made it impossible. She tapped the light and as it turned on again, I could see she was holding a slender rectangle with a half-naked man on it. Good to know I hadn't lost my phone. We were barely in a cavern big enough to hold us. It was by sheer luck we hadn't been crushed when the building toppled. Before I could turn around and inspect the rubble, the light sputtered again.

The boy inched closer, pressing against my side. He lacked his companion's bravery as he shook. I didn't know what to fear more, being crushed to death, running out of oxygen, or the moment they asked if the tooth fairy was real.

I pulled the boy close, wrapping my arm around him. "We'll be okay. We just have to stay calm."

"I am calm." The girl's confidence knew no bounds. I was almost envious of her certainty that we'd survive this. Oh, to be a child again.

"I know a lot of superheroes. They're going to be looking for me."

"You do?" The boy's voice had dropped to a mumble. I suspected he was terrified of the dark. I wasn't too thrilled either, kiddo.

"My phone, I need it." I held out my hand, waiting for the girl to hand it over. She debated giving away the only source of light. I wrapped my arm around the boy, pulling him close before snatching the phone out of her hand. I wouldn't stop a ton of concrete from crushing us, but I wasn't giving up hope yet.

There were a lot of superheroes in my phone book. But this wasn't a lonely night requiring a warm body in my bed. There were several good candidates, but only one who could make it here in seconds and drag us to safety.

A: Need evac. Trapped in a collapsed building near HideOut.

I stared at the text message. The kids watched closely, and I prayed that a dick pic didn't flash across my screen. The last thing I needed was to scar the children before the building flattened us.

T: ...

Three dots appeared and promptly vanished.

"You're being ignored," said the girl. I was about to type when the screen went black. The red battery light flashed before leaving us in a perfect black.

"Great," I mumbled. The boy scooted closer, practically crawling into my lap. I was about to tell him everything would be fine when a roar ripped through the building. I grabbed the girl and pulled her tight, rolling on top of the kids.

Dust filled the space as I growled, preparing for the weight of the building to break me in half. Both kids screamed. Seconds later, it was over. They were alive. I was alive. We were all alive.

"We're okay," I said, hoping I didn't jinx our survival. The echo in the room had vanished. Whatever had fallen had cut the space in half, and if the debris shifted again, we wouldn't survive.

"Where's your friend?" I did not impress her in the least. But it was the same question I asked myself. It's not as if I casually sent Theo text messages to rescue me from certain doom. It was bad enough to be ignored by a hero. Fine, they had to save the world. But my boyfriend ignoring a desperate plea to prevent my imminent death? We'd be exchanging words.

"I'll get us out of here." I had little faith in the statement, but everybody needed to hear the lie. If I could move some of the debris, the kids might be small enough to climb to safety. But what rock? Where did I start? Or was it better to sit and wait and hope somebody came to our rescue?

I pounded against the wall, searching for an echo that might suggest a hollow space. But with an entire building resting above us, it was fruitless. I wasn't going to be the hero of the story. If I died, I was going to be seriously pissed at Theo.

"Find an exit?" Her superpower was the smug satisfaction in which she hinted at an 'I told you so.'

I resisted the urge to smother the girl. At the rate things were going, the building would kill us. If my patience wasn't earning my way into Heaven, I was going to be irked. I deserved the VIP treatment.

Rumbling started from somewhere high above us. The boy whimpered and even the smart-mouthed girl curled into a ball as I braced. It grew louder, and at any moment, it'd rip through the ground and we'd be crushed. Even if we survived, the dust filling the air made it difficult to breathe. I didn't want to die, especially not from suffocation. The thought compounded as I thought of the kids. I tried to cover as much of them as my body allowed. I couldn't save them, but if I bought them another minute, it might be enough time for a hero to arrive.

The sound grew louder and the surrounding cement shifted. I held my breath, less from the dust and more to prepare for the excruciating pain about to consume my body. I hoped it'd happen quickly, for all our sakes.

The dust vanished, sucked from the space as light poured in. It was so bright that I couldn't make out the hero holding a cement slab over his head. The barrel-chested man tossed it to the side as if it were an empty cardboard box. I was relieved he had gotten my—

"You're safe now." It wasn't the burly bear I expected. I

hoped it was EO coming to my rescue, but I wouldn't turn away the familiar voice.

"Sentinel, get them. They might need medical attention."

"I'm fine, no thanks to you." I was too tired to ask Bernard to put the cement back and bury her alive.

Rolling over, I revealed my bunkmates. Bernard's face shone as he turned. With a wave of his arm, Zipper appeared. The Ward's speedster swooped in, picking up the kids, and in a flash, they vanished. At least I wouldn't have to listen to her chastise my lack of superpowers.

"Are you hurt?"

Bernard took my hand, lifting me from the rubble as if I weighed nothing. "Only my ego. Kids can be so mean."

"We can go find Griffin, and I'll drop you off."

"No," I said, waving him off. "Go save the city, Papi. I'll be fine."

He didn't argue. Bernard gave my shoulder a pat before he turned around, showing off the battle ax strapped to his back. I never understood why he chose that of all the weapons he could use as a superhero, or why he used a weapon at all.

Lightning erupted from his body, striking the ground. Up he went, flying into the sky before changing directions and heading into danger. I was thankful for the save, but I couldn't hide the disappointment that it wasn't the man I expected. I didn't want to treat Theo like a booty call whenever I got into trouble, but part of me hoped it came with the package.

Right now, I wanted to get back to my apartment, plug in my phone, and see if he responded to my text. I prayed that something horrible hadn't happened. For now, I needed to find Griffin and make sure he survived the attack. Once I found him, we could start scouring the alleys for survivors. The heroes might stop the baddies, but even those of us without powers had a civic duty to help.

I checked my phone, verifying it was dead. First, be a Good Samaritan, then I'd find out why Theo ignored my message.

19

———

"THERE'S ALWAYS TOKYO. I KNOW A LITTLE HOLE-IN-THE-wall place with the best sushi."

I was running on almost no sleep. Griffin, Chad, and I had organized a search party, going through the buildings near the battle, searching for survivors. Each time we heard somebody crying for help, out came Griffin's phone to report it to the heroes. The destruction wasn't anything abnormal, but usually villains were polite enough to wait for civilians to be home before destroying the city. Thankfully, they were rarely concerned with obliterating mankind.

I eyed the sign above the door "Golden Dragon Emerald Palace Great Wall." It couldn't be any more Americanized if they screamed, "We have chicken nuggets." But

173

right now, I wanted a quiet place with comfort food. The pork fried rice and imitation crab rangoons were the hug my body needed. If I didn't pack away the food now, I would never survive a night at the bar.

Bernard demanded I go to the hospital. Nothing had been broken, but the doctor promised plenty of bruising. I had grabbed my power cable on the way back to the Hide-Out, where Chad was sweeping glass. The last few hours had been securing wood to the windows until his insurance paid for replacements.

"Thanks, but maybe another night. I need mundane right now. Boring. I crave boring."

Theo raised an eyebrow. "I'm not sure how I should take that."

"Not you," I patted him on the chest before giving him a kiss. It was adorable that he was wearing a t-shirt with a comic book superhero on it. The irony wasn't lost on me. "You can stay sexy." I flashed a smile. "But can you be a boring sexy?"

The little fob in my hand vibrated, signaling that our table had been cleared. "I don't know how you do it all the time. One emergency to the next. I'm ready to sleep for a week."

Theo opened the door with a sweeping bow. A young woman smiled, taking the fob before leading us to our table. With only twenty seats in the restaurant, even on its busiest night, it never got loud. I should have called out of work for the night. But between date night with Theo and wanting to hear gossip about the Nocturnals, I couldn't sit on the couch without feeling like I was missing out.

"The union makes sure we take our sick leave."

I raised an eyebrow. "Wait, there's a union?"

He laughed. "Of course. If it wasn't for them, how would we negotiate healthcare plans? Half of our members require specialized care." He leaned in, whispering. "Do you know how difficult it is to draw blood from a man with skin made of steel?"

I hadn't given it much thought. Xander always complained about having to sort out a super's powers before saving them from death. I hadn't considered that it came with a price tag. These people were saving the city from destruction and we couldn't pay for their band-aids? Their problems weren't so different from the rest of us.

Theo picked up the menu and browsed while weighing in on the newest villains of Vanguard. "The Nocturnals are really making a mess of this city. Who knew five people could be so difficult to take down?"

Superheroes would always be the primary discussion when dating a man with powers. Your only option to avoid it was to move to a place like Sleepy City, Kansas. Nobody wanted that.

"They went from nobodies to somebodies really quick.

There's still no clue who they are or what they're after. It's almost like their goal is to cause chaos. They evaded the Centurions. I'm betting they're a bunch of jerks living in their mothers' basements."

I chuckled at the image as Theo theorized about the Nocturnal's origin story.

"And if the Centurions can't stop them..." I let the worry drift into the open.

I wondered if Bernard had an opinion on it. Now that his alter ego was out in the open, could I press him for details? Papi couldn't resist telling me the juicy bits. I nearly squealed at the thought of watching his face flush as I asked him about what superhero antics he got into when the suit hit the floor.

Theo set his phone on the table, giving it a quick glance. I half expected to catch a glance of the HeroApp™, but it looked like he had his texts open. Did the heroes always have their phones handy, ready to jump into danger? The idea of always being "on" made me sad for them. I was used to having sexy time cut short as they had to save the city, but knowing it was a burden that they and the people in their lives couldn't avoid... That felt daunting.

"Being trapped under that building was probably the scariest thing that's ever happened to me. It didn't help that one of the kids I saved kept reminding me I wasn't doing an outstanding job."

"What were you thinking?" Theo asked. "You could have been crushed."

"It wasn't exactly my plan. Running and hiding with Griffin and Chad was the goal. But then I heard the kids screaming. I couldn't leave them behind, and before I could get Griffin to help, he vanished in a cloud of rubble." I was thankful there were only a few scratches, but the ache had already started working its way into my bones. Tylenol and a hot bath would not cut it tonight.

"I tried texting you, but my phone died."

"The reports hadn't come in yet. I thought you were joking."

I caught my breath, trying to keep my lips from frowning. He had received the text? I had been stuck underneath a building, risking my life saving two munchkins, and he thought I was joking. It was bad enough when Griffin ignored my GIFs of sexy men saving puppies. But to be ignored when I could have died?

I was about to lay out the guilt when the waitress appeared. While Theo ordered half a dozen rolls of sushi, my attention turned from being ignored to the rumbling in my stomach. I'd bring it up later, but right now, all I wanted to do was stuff my face.

Try as I might to focus on the upcoming feast, the nagging disappointment rivaled my desire for raw fish. Keeping my thoughts to myself had never been my strong suit. But if I didn't say it now…

"I almost died. A building nearly crushed me. If it hadn't been for Sentinel, at best, I'd still be stuck down there. At worst…" I let the words trail off. It almost felt foolish putting the thought into the universe. Living in Vanguard City meant the constant threat of being killed by villains with a grudge. But this wasn't a flashy bad guy trying to get revenge. It was me trying to be a good person and almost paying the price. More than that, the one person I needed at that moment had thought I was being dramatic.

Theo reached across the table, wrapping his hands around mine. His thumb ran across my knuckles. I wanted to relish the feeling, to let my heart thump against my ribs as this handsome man turned his focus on me. I had been worried that sharing him with Julian would be complicated and that I wouldn't be able to compete with their marriage. But Julian didn't factor into the reasons my chest ached. When I needed Theo the most, he ignored me.

"I can't imagine what was going through your head." His words were slow, deliberate as he tread carefully through the minefield I had laid. "I'm sorry. This one is on me. I should have been there."

I get it. He wasn't my personal savior. I didn't have a monopoly on this hero, and he couldn't be there to save me every time I found myself in danger. I didn't need him to be my everything. I needed him to be my *something*.

"You ignored my text." I caught the sob in my throat. This wasn't the date I had planned. It should have a little romance, maybe some staring across the table, and end with me dragging him into the bedroom. Instead, this dinner for two invited my insecurities as a third wheel.

"I can apologize all day for that, but it doesn't change what I did. Alejandro, you didn't deserve that. If you'll forgive me." He paused as his phone vibrated. I expected him to pick it up and make sure the world wasn't burning.

"It won't happen again."

He maintained eye contact. They were the softest pools of blue. How many arguments had he escaped with them? I wanted to forgive him, to allow it to become a misunderstanding that we grew from. The logic rattling around inside my brain didn't convince my heart. The two remained at odds even as I nodded my head and smiled.

"Sorry," I said, "dinner wasn't supposed to be a guilt trip."

"I hurt your feelings," he jumped in. "Never keep your feelings bottled up. I'm mad at myself for being *that* guy. You have nothing to apologize for."

Validation. It didn't solve the problem, but it put a band-aid on the wound so it could heal. It wasn't perfect, but it was a start. As he squeezed my hands, I realized I hadn't felt this way about a person in a long time. All the time spent naked with the heroes from Midnight Alley, I hadn't considered opening myself to the possibility of something other than a tryst. Something about Theo broke down my walls, but without defenses, I feared I was preparing for a world of pain.

His phone vibrated again. I swore it grew angrier, shaking about the table as if it were throwing a tantrum. "Are you going to get that?"

Theo kept one hand stretched across the table, locked around my fingers as if he were attempting to save me from falling off a building. He picked up the phone and flicked at the screen with his thumb. I recognized the expression, the furrowed brow and the slight downturn of the lip. Duty called, and as a protector of the city, he couldn't say no. It was the burden of being a superhero's trophy husband.

"If you need to go—"

"I'd much rather be here with you."

"Duty calls," I said. "The other mistress." Well, I guess in this case, it was one of several. I'd have to work out the details on that.

"Be right back. I'm going to pay."

"You don't—"

"I've been enough of a jerk today."

He jumped from the table and I half expected him to step into a portal to hunt down our waitress. He vanished toward the entrance while his phone continued to vibrate violently. I picked it up, ready to shout for Theo that his little box of doom demanded attention. But he had turned the corner to pay the tab.

"Man, and I thought my phone got used and abused."

I spun it around to see where the HeroApp™ would take him. The notifications on the Lock Screen weren't from an app. They were texts. I hadn't imagined the heroes passed out their numbers and activated the phone tree when danger struck. It seemed like an inefficient way to—

The phone shook again, a message popping up on the screen.

Julian: Whatever you are doing, drop it. I need you here, now."

The wound re-opened. I sent a text message before death came knocking and I got ignored. But Julian sends an S.O.S. and Theo jumps into action. I might have Theo's attention, but it appeared he only offered it when convenient. I didn't want to cause a scene. It wasn't hurt pumping through my veins, it was anger. I was thankful he was leaving, so I could stew in my misery.

Theo returned to the table. I handed him his phone, and he leaned in, kissing me on the forehead. "Consider this a rain check. I'll make it up to you."

He glanced in both directions before opening a portal and vanishing. I felt foolish as I sat there by myself. It was only amplified as the waitress arrived, setting down three plates of food. It looked delicious, but suddenly, I wasn't hungry.

She asked if I needed anything else, and I blinked as I processed the question. I hadn't been aware at the time, but there was something I needed, and as Theo vanished for whatever emergency awaited him, I knew the answer to the question.

I needed *more*.

20

My usual workplace flare had vanished. I mixed the martini with a single shake before dumping the liquid into a glass. I feigned a smile as I pushed it across the table, dropping in an olive without a toothpick. The hero eyed the drink before setting down the exact change. I couldn't blame her for ignoring the tip.

"Why so solemn?"

It was as if the gods above were determined to test my patience. I cursed under my breath as Eclipse took a seat at the bar. Normally, I'd spin around the conversation, taking my jabs with uncanny precision. But tonight, I didn't want to play games. I wanted to do my job, close out the bar, and go to sleep. It was by sheer force of will that I came into work. Eclipse would have to survive without getting a reaction.

"What do you want?"

He looked behind the bar, studying the hundred bottles as if he knew what to order. The white mask hiding his face made it impossible to tell where his eyes were pointing. Like every time he waltzed into the bar, it looked as if he had picked up his suit from the dry cleaners. For a man who refused to use his powers to protect the city, he certainly acted like we owed him. My dislike for Eclipse turned to hate.

I didn't wait for the reply. On a good day, I couldn't tolerate him, and now I wanted the man gone.

I grabbed a bottle off the shelf and started mixing. "A hero chaser it is." If my martini had been lackluster, this was downright appalling. If Scarlet caught me mixing drinks like a rookie, she'd take me by the ear and drag me to the floor like mi madre.

"And here I thought *you* were the hero chaser." Eclipse acted as if my reputation was a well-guarded secret. Anybody who set foot in the bar knew that on a good day, I'd flirt, and if they were burly, they'd stand a chance of making it to my bedroom. I didn't hide my extracurricular activities. I was a slut and never ashamed to admit it.

"For *actual* heroes, maybe."

Neither of us budged. A staring contest. I might not be able to take him in an arm-wrestling contest. Or maybe I could? Eclipse hadn't shown off his powers. I learned that if they weren't open with their abilities, they weren't worth mentioning. With this petulant man-child, I bet the same could be said about his *other* attributes.

Eclipse turned, as if he were looking for a friend in the bar. Victory. Childish, I know, but it was that or I'd throw a drink in his face. It'd fast-track, ending my night. I'm not sure Scarlet would let me come back, but with her leaving, was that a bad thing?

"When I own this operation—"

"Are you about to make an idle threat?"

"I wouldn't quite say, idle."

His cheeks rose, creating an eerie smile visible through his mask. I couldn't believe that Scarlet considered giving her baby away to this asshole. Estás pero si bien pendejo. She and I were going to have a talk before the night ended.

"We'll have to have a heart-to-heart when I'm your boss."

Did Eclipse really have the funds to purchase the club outright? Was it a done deal? I thought back to the many times the two of them had talked. Were there no other rich heroes looking for an investment opportunity? Even with her need to retire, I couldn't believe she'd be willing to put this jerk in charge. The bar wouldn't last a year under his management.

"Who knows? Maybe we can get to know one another outside the bar?"

I slammed the tumbler onto the bar, splashing the cocktail across the front of my shirt. The man had insulted me, threatened my job, and now he was propositioning me? I couldn't figure out what Eclipse wanted. Did he walk into a room to spread chaos? Cause right now, I couldn't pinpoint the purpose of this exchange.

"You think I'd be interested in seeing you if I wasn't being paid?"

"Money won't be an issue."

He offered to buy my time? I didn't know if I should be offended or honored that he considered me worthy of the wad of cash crumpled in his wallet. The sex workers probably turned away his money.

"I have standards." I poured the drink into a martini glass. "And *you* do not make the cut. I'd rather quit than work for a wannabe like you. You can't buy my dignity."

I set the glass on the counter. For him, I neglected to wipe it down, and he'd be damned if I was including an orange wedge. In fact, I didn't want his money now.

"It's on the house. Asshole's delight."

Eclipse pulled back his mask, lifting the cowl high enough to expose his mouth and mustache. He devoured the drink, throwing it back like a professional. I hope he choked.

"Without this job," he whispered, "you'll be nothing."

I reached out, flipping my middle finger in his direction. Before I could revel in the shock on his face, he grabbed my hand. I tried to pull away, but what he lacked in manners, he made up in strength.

"Worthless," he said.

I imagined reaching into the cooler, grabbing a beer, and smashing the bottle on the counter. I couldn't match his strength, but I could find out if he could bleed. For a moment, it was as if the world turned dark. The lights in Midnight Alley vanished like they had shut the power off. Eclipse's suit, however, maintained its vibrant white, almost glowing. But he let go of my hand and stepped backward, allowing the shadows to swallow him.

"What the hell?"

In the distance, I could see an image push through the darkness. It was Theo, and... me? We were sitting at the table from earlier in the evening. As he got up, I watched as I picked up his phone. It was like watching my life through a television screen. Worst yet, of all the shows I could watch, why this one?

"Oh? My fling? Don't worry, he won't get in the way."

Theo's voice echoed in the void. I had never heard him say that before, but it was certainly how it felt when I saw the message. The insecurity buried in the back of my head had been exhumed and laid out in the open.

"He's a temporary distraction at best."

"No," I whispered. "No. No. No." I shook my head, trying to change the channel. It was horrible to think these thoughts, but to have them confirmed? There was no point in hiding the tears.

It was replaced with a crumbling building. I recognized

it, the same one I had run into for the kids. I couldn't fathom what Eclipse had done to make these images surface. Maybe he was a telepath, and he was poking around in my head for details about my life?

"I wish a real hero would save us." The girl's voice taunted me.

"We'll have to make do," said the boy.

"Alejandro, you're wasting my time." Even Bernard's voice cut through the darkness. "There are people who deserve to be saved."

Before I could process the voices, a solitary man stood in the vast emptiness. It appeared as if a streetlamp shone downward, making the outer edges of his hoodie glow a soft orange. The width of the figure combined with the white skull on his t-shirt and bright red sneakers... I gasped.

"Dan?"

He stepped further into the light, letting the red in his beard shine. It had been years since I had seen him, but he hadn't aged a minute. Despite the distance between us, he was never far from my thoughts. Bernard claimed I let him live rent-free in my head. Truth be told, he had free rein in the asylum most days. I thought it had changed with Theo, but I was only one bad day from thinking about the man who crushed my heart.

"Dan, is that you?"

"You know the answer to that. How could you forget the best thing that ever happened to you?"

When I beat myself up or my self-confidence plummeted, it was the worry I focused on. Dan had been wonderful—at first. But somewhere along the line, he made every argument my fault. It reached a point where he managed to gaslight me at every turn, making me doubt my sanity. I thought those days were behind me.

"You changed. You're not the man I fell in love with," I said.

"If that's what you have to tell yourself. But let's be honest with ourselves. You sabotaged our relationship. I would have given you the world, but you forced me out. I didn't want to leave. You made me."

Was he right? Had I ruined everything?

"Are you okay? Alejandro, you vanished for a moment."

The music came rushing in as Eclipse let go of my hand. My eyes adjusted to the overhead lights as he pushed his mask into place. I shook my head, trying to shake the cold sensation clinging to my skin. The tears reached my cheeks before I wiped them away.

"Don't get lost in thought while on the job. I wouldn't want to fire the Alley's best bartender."

Eclipse turned around and walked into the crowd. Is this what a mental breakdown felt like? My chest heaved, but more than that, my heart ached as I tried to convince myself that none of it had been real. In the rubble, the kids never said that, nor had Bernard. At least, I didn't think so. But Theo, on the other hand, I wanted to believe he wouldn't say those words aloud. But did he think them? The fear of the truth threatened to force out the tears again.

Damn you, Eclipse.

21

A: How'd heroing go?

Sanity deserted me. I stared at the phone on the bar, trying to imagine the rational reasons Theo hadn't responded. He could be saving the world or helping a little old lady cross the road. Perhaps he fell asleep? There were a thousand reasons he couldn't reply, all of them reasonable. Then why did I keep staring at the message?

"How'd heroing go? It's straightforward, right?" What if it was too casual? Like it didn't say, respond now, I'm sort of freaking out. Or worse, what if he thought I was being intrusive? He didn't have to report every time he saved the world. No, that'd be foolish.

It'd only be a matter of seconds before I spiraled into an anxiety attack. I didn't want Theo to know how far under my skin Eclipse had gotten. With a few simple words, he had me daydreaming about an unconfirmed conspiracy. Could this be my brain and heart having a conflict? They could be duking it out, and right now, I'm pretty sure my heart was being trampled. Had I been fooling myself this entire time?

A: Papi, you up?

I needed a voice of reason. He might be capable of wielding lightning like a God, but Bernard's superpower was cutting through my hysterics.

B: Still not being your booty call.

With a single text, my papa bear left me smiling. I could spend hours texting him about nothing. He'd gripe about how it'd be faster as a phone call, but he'd entertain my refusal to pick up his calls. But right now, I needed him to reach through the phone and brush aside my insecurities. Drowning in my crumbling self-confidence, I needed him to save me for the second time today.

A: ...

What could I say that didn't sound desperate?

B: Al, is everything okay?

A: I'm having a rough night.

B: *hugs* Here if you need me.

B: ... mi osito.

Little bear. Just like that, Bernard typed exactly what I needed to hear. I couldn't help but let out a slight sob with the laugh. It eased the pressure in my chest. Unlike Theo, Bernard didn't hide.

My pity party was cut short as the music scratched to a halt. Across the club, in the round booths that faced the stage, Scarlet remained frozen, her arm extended, ending in a fist. Eclipse's face was half turned. She stood, shaking her hand, threatening to repeat the maneuver.

"Did Scarlet just punch Eclipse?"

Bruno took a seat at the bar, not wanting to miss the action. I couldn't blame him. For all the years I had worked here, I had never seen Scarlet resort to violence. But as she rocked her weight backward, keeping her gait narrow and fists raised, it appeared there was no taking the hero out of the heroine.

"Girl, do it again," I begged. "In fact, tell him I requested the next punch."

"I guess this means she's not selling the club." Bruno had a point. Unless there was a weird custom between heroes where they punched one another instead of offering a hearty handshake, the deal appeared off the table. I wouldn't celebrate until she revealed her backup plan, but anything would be better than working for Eclipse.

The crowd didn't cheer, but by the expressions from the room, they were all thinking the same thing. It was the first time I noticed a collective distaste for Eclipse and his band of sycophants. I knew there was a reason I poured heavy when making their drinks. Would it be in poor taste to buy a round for the house to celebrate?

Eclipse's cronies had jumped to their feet. In a room

full of heroes, fights almost never happened. Even when egos were wounded, a nearby sidekick would swoop in to save the day.

"Should we do something?" I asked.

"What do I look like?" He stopped for a moment and laughed. Bruno remained our bouncer in name only. "Nope, still not happening. The boss can handle herself."

Eclipse jumped to his feet, yelling at Scarlet. But his tantrum did nothing to scare the woman. Her stance relaxed as it became obvious he wouldn't retaliate.

"Shit, he's coming over."

Bruno turned around on his bar stool, attempting to hide his interest in the show. Me however, I wanted Eclipse to know I had seen every moment. In fact, if I had recorded it, I'd play it again as I laughed. My love life might be imploding, but I could put that aside long enough to watch my arch-nemesis snarl in disgust.

"Is somebody having a rough night?"

"Whisky, straight."

I flipped a glass onto the table. Grabbing a bottle off the shelf, I made sure the smile reached from ear to ear. I poured heavy, happy to take it out of my tips for the night. He pulled at the cowl, raising it far enough that he could gulp his drink.

"Do you need a hug? Maybe we can go somewhere and talk? You know, as your future employee."

He lifted the glass, but it shattered in his hand. The growl came from deep in his gut, and at any moment, I thought he might lunge across the counter. Thankfully, I was in a room with a hundred superheroes, ready to put the man in his place.

"Do you need another, future boss?"

Eclipse slammed his fist down on the bar, breaking off a chunk. The room continued watching, with several heroes stepping forward should I need their services. I held up my hand, signaling for them to stay put.

"You," he snarled, "and this bar can go to hell."

He was getting a taste of his own medicine. "If you forgot where the door is, I'll gladly show you."

"Not yet." The scowl stretched across his face until he smiled, baring his teeth. "I'm still waiting for somebody."

How did you tell a flunky that nobody at the bar would go home with him? Is there proper etiquette? Or do you tear off the band-aid, hoping that it doesn't tear the skin? After our earlier exchange, I'd tear him apart any which way I could.

"I'd keep you company, but I don't want to disappoint my current—"

"Alejandro?"

Eclipse laughed. "Oh, I think you know my friend."

Even with Bruno blocking my view of the door, I recognized the voice. It only took a single word, and it transported me to the worst period in my life. One word and the walls stopped crumbling. Now they exploded in a fury of anger and what if's.

"Dan?" Bruno leaned to the side, and there he stood, almost exactly as he had in Eclipse's freakish broadcast. The years had been good to him, deepening his laugh lines and thickening his biceps. I had a thousand questions that were never answered when he left. But we had to start somewhere.

"What are you doing here?"

Eclipse leaned across the bar, whispering loud enough to say it was for show. "Oh, did I forget to mention I had a date? If you weren't going to take me up on my offer, I thought I should reach out to somebody who'd appreciate my company."

Fingernails bit into my palms as I curled my fingers into a fist. Scarlet wouldn't be the only one to knock the spit out of the wannabe hero.

Eclipse's voice dropped, now whispering just for me. "You make it too easy, Alejandro. The fear is palpable. You don't need me stoking the flames. You're doing a fine job of self-destructing."

I swung. When Scarlet fired me, it'd be worth it. None of the heroes came to his rescue. No speedsters caught my fist. No mind controllers halted my muscles. As my knuckles drilled into his chin, I prepared the other fist, ready to follow it with another strike. The second fist stopped short as Eclipse caught my hand.

"Maybe I should leave the two of you to talk."

He acted as if he hadn't dropped a bomb. He motioned to his entourage and only stopped to give Dan a pat on the shoulder. Eclipse had gone from a nuisance to a target for my rage. I wanted nothing more than to pound away at the man's face until it turned into a bloody pulp.

"I didn't know," Dan said as he approached the bar. "Promise."

"You good?" Bruno had raised an eyebrow, trying to decide if he'd be needed or if he should give us privacy. I gave him a slight nod, and he returned to the door.

"What are you doing with that arrogant playboy?"

"Seems I have a type."

Did Dan just compare me to Eclipse? There were a lot of insults I could handle, but I was nothing like that asshole. I had to remind myself that Dan wasn't much better than his supposed date. It wouldn't surprise me if this was another attempt to gaslight. Eclipse did have one thing right. No matter how hard I tried to push Dan from my mind, he always teetered on the edge of my thoughts.

"He's using you. That guy is an asshole."

"You're not one to speak. I seem to remember you being quite the asshole. I thought we were happy, and then I found out you were out whoring around town with anybody wearing a cape."

"A rumor." My jaw clenched. I couldn't let him get under my skin. It was his superpower, and it'd eat me alive if I let it. "I'm sure you started it to keep your superior image."

"You haven't changed. You can't take responsibility. Everybody told me I should leave you. But I didn't listen. They told me you were a slut with no self-control. I thought you had changed."

He threw his hands up in the air, done with the conversation. Dan turned around, heading to the door. "You haven't changed, Al." He shoved Bruno out of the way and exited the club.

The room remained silent, all eyes focused on me. While they had appeared joyous that I attempted to clobber Eclipse, their expressions dripped with pity. Even Scarlet pointed to the DJ and cued the music. The heroes returned to their circles, stealing casual glances at the poor bartender as I repeated Dan's last words.

"I had changed," I mumbled. "For you."

Something inside broke.

22

———————

"Go home, Alejandro."

Scarlet restrained from using her gifts. She didn't have to coerce me with her powers. As the boss, the words came with authority, and she wasn't in a mood to be challenged.

I nodded. "Sorry, Scarlet. I let you down."

Furiously, she shook her head. She put a hand on my chin, forcing me to stare her in the eye. Their softness didn't match her tone. Pulling me close for a hug, she squeezed hard enough that she lifted me off the ground. I forgot she could bend steel, and my spine, by the feel of it.

"You take care of yourself. Eclipse lashed out like a sore loser. You don't have to worry. I doubt we'll see him in here much after that."

"But what about—"

"Shh," she put a finger over my lips. "We'll talk about

everything later. Right now, I want my best bartender to go home and take care of himself."

If the weight of the world hadn't landed on my shoulders all at once, her words would have made me smile. Now, it was all I could do to not cry at the sincerity of her concern. She turned me around and pushed me toward the door.

"I'll see you tomorrow, Alejandro. Try not to be late."

We both knew I'd ignore her request.

Bruno pushed the metal door open, stepping to the side like a gentleman. He gave me a swift slap on the ass as I headed out. "My hero. Maybe next time, I'll get a lick in."

I waved to the man as I turned down the street. "Adios, Bruno."

At least there were a few people in my life that didn't think I was a horrible human being. According to Dan, it'd only be a matter of time before they caught on. After our breakup, the one he says I caused, our social circle fell apart. Nobody returned phone calls and plans were canceled. Part of me worried it was only a matter of time before Griffin or Xander stopped responding.

I wanted to believe it wouldn't happen again, that I had learned my lesson. Yet, I continued checking my phone to see if Theo had responded to my text. Could he be another Dan? Getting my hopes up and breaking down my walls just so he could reach through a portal and tear out my heart?

"Stop it," I chided myself.

I had reached the subway when a gust of wind blew past. I expected to see a streak as the Zipper ran past on another superhero call. But the road was almost empty, only drunk couples stumbling from bars into cabs.

"You're paranoid, Al."

In grade school, we all went through supervillain survival. Every first grader knew ways to keep themselves safe. By fifth grade, the teachers were teaching nuanced safety tips to keep us out of danger. The most important: Trust your gut. If something feels wrong, it *is* wrong. In Vanguard City, it could be the difference between life and death.

The hair on my arms stood on end. It wasn't *if* something weird happened; it became *when*. Only an idiot would be dumb enough to attack a civilian this close to the Alley.

Thankfully, the skies were empty, meaning a flier wouldn't snatch me off the street. But in a city, it didn't matter. Villains also loved to jump out from buildings as if they were playing a sadistic game of peek-a-boo. I stepped away from the sewer grate. Nobody wanted to be dragged underneath the city when the Moleman went hunting for a new bride.

"I know you're there," I whispered. Maybe if they didn't hear me, they'd go away.

Something in a nearby alley caused a bang. Nope, no

more waiting. I made a break for it. If they wanted to kidnap me, they'd have to deal with a moving target. I cursed myself for skipping leg day... for skipping gym day altogether.

There were feet striking the pavement, following. Not one set, but many. I didn't dare turn around to see how far away they were. Chased by villains and not a single hero in sight. Hell, at this point, I'd take a well-intentioned Boy Scout.

"Help!" Maybe a hero exiting the club had super hearing. I only needed one person to jump in and give me time to run away.

I rounded the corner, ducking into the entrance of a shop. With the door pressed against my back, I prayed they ran past without giving me a second glance. I expected to see hooligans, maybe hooligans with capes, but nobody rounded the corner and ran past.

Perhaps it had been—

Glass shattered as hands grabbed my shoulders, pulling me through the front door of the shop. I barely noticed the wedding dress in the window before being tossed across the floor. Shielding my eyes, I didn't dare risk the broken glass in my face as the attacker pulled me to my feet by my tie.

"What were you hiding from? Me?"

I recognized the voice. Yet again, the leader of the Nocturnals treated me as his personal plaything. He lifted me off my feet, plowing me backward until he had me pinned between two white dresses. With a swift kick to his gut, he hardly flinched. My back ached as he slammed me against the wall again. Being buried alive had left plenty of bruises, and now this jerk was filling in the gaps with new ones.

"Feisty, aren't we?"

"What do you want? No little old ladies to pick on?" It probably wasn't smart to antagonize a man capable of breaking me in half, but some lessons took longer to sink in.

The featureless white mask came in close, like he was sniffing me. I had been around enough heroes to know some of them enjoyed their scents. Who am I to judge? But right now was not the time for fetish play.

"Self-doubt."

"Great, you stated the obvious. Is that your power?" I reached into my pocket, trying to grab my phone. If I could hit the volume button enough, it'd signal the HeroApp™ that something was amiss. I only needed to—

"No heroes are saving you." He pulled my hand out of my pants and pinned it to the wall. "You're not worthy of being saved. Even Sentinel thought so. He'd have left you to rot if not for the kids."

How did he— Wait, was that anxiety attack earlier not real? Could it have been...

"Eclipse."

The mask melted away from his skin. I didn't recognize the man until the smile formed under his mustache, teeth bared, almost as white as his suit. I wouldn't have thought the man stupid enough to show up at Midnight Alley in a white suit and then terrorize the city in an identical color. The pattern on his chest and arms had changed, but it didn't require a genius to figure it out. Though, in a city where skimpy masks hid a person's identity, he had done more than most. Worst off, it worked. From now on, I'd start paying more attention.

"You're one of the Nocturnals?"

"If I made it any more obvious, I'd have a name tag. It's only a matter of time before we achieve our goal and the city rests under the heel of my boot."

In the bar, that hadn't been me, not entirely. Eclipse could draw out fear to manifest it until it consumed his victim. Even now, he attempted to get in my head. The doubts and insecurities attempted to push past my common sense. Sentinel, annoyed as he hovered above the fallen building, flashed across my mind. I wouldn't let it take hold. Instead, I focused on the image of a burly man sitting in his living room, texting with me. Ha, try again Eclipse. His powers would not get their claws in me again.

"Bravado?" Had I surprised the man? I might not be faster than a speeding train, but I'd resist his prodding with every ounce of energy I could muster.

"You're just as bad a villain as you are a hero." It all

made sense now, the immaculate uniform, elbowing it with the heroes at the club. He wasn't trying to climb the social ladder. He and his crew were gathering intel.

"I let you have the first hit free. But next time, it's going to cost you. And with your track record, there isn't going to be anybody left to save you from the big bad wolf."

"Sentinel will—"

"No, EO? Did you already burn that bridge?"

The shop turned black like it had in the subway. Eclipse was about to use his powers to pull at my worst fears. How do you protect yourself against fear? No amount of self-confidence could bat away the insecurities lying just beneath the surface.

"Oh, I see." He feigned sympathy, driving the dagger deeper into my heart. "He got bored with his distraction? Found somebody better? More deserving? I can't say I blame him. I hear you're fun..." He leaned in, his lips grazing my ear. "For an evening."

With a flick of the wrist, he released his grip, tossing me into a row of mannequins. I scurried away, trying to reach the door before Eclipse pulled at my ankles and hurled me into the street.

"I suppose I should take my cue from EO. You're not worth the effort. You'll self-destruct all on your own."

I climbed to my feet, prepared to run before daring to glance over my shoulder. The shop was still, and there was no man in white to be found. It shouldn't surprise me that

Eclipse wanted to terrorize me, especially after I clocked him.

But he wasn't wrong. It wasn't his powers that had shaken me. My issues with Theo had started before Eclipse got involved. Could he really create fear? Or did it have to be grounded in reality? Not knowing was the most unnerving part of it. I tried to blame the pain in my chest on the arrogant prick. And yet, I couldn't help imagining Theo silencing his phone when my message came in, placing me at the bottom of his priorities.

"I can't do this," I mumbled. The phone was in my hand, and before I knew it, I was staring at the text message I had sent earlier. Part of me hoped I missed his reply, anything to give me pause. With a simple, "Got tied up," I'd be able to scream at Eclipse that he lost. But it had been hours and still no word from Theo. On its own, it wouldn't have been a big deal, but after dinner, and him mistaking a plea for help as overreacting... I didn't like the man I had become. Worse than that, I didn't like the sinking feeling threatening to swallow me whole.

A: I can't do this.

Then I clicked send.

23

———

IT WAS TOO LATE TO CALL GRIFFIN, AND I DIDN'T WANT TO listen to him compare my situation to his perfect relationship with Sebastian. Xander would be asleep, most likely with Aiden. Then there was Bernard, our perpetual stag. I stared at my phone, reading his last text.

"Mi osito."

I didn't want to message him again. It was one thing to reach out for assurance, but I didn't want him worrying. Tomorrow, over breakfast, I'd tell them what happened and let them go into detail about what kind of idiot I had been. But tonight, I wanted to stew in my misery. I deserved nothing less.

I stared at the message to Theo. Seconds after sending it, I blocked his number to stop myself from taking it back. I didn't want to hear his explanation. Eclipse might be nothing more than a villain terrorizing the city, but he hadn't been wrong. I was burning bridges as I went. It was bad enough that I felt like they had blown a hole in my chest, first by Dan, then Theo, and Dan again. It was time to walk away from the situation before my suspicions were confirmed.

The phone dinged and my heart jumped. There was no way it was Theo, but somehow, I wanted to see a message coming from a blocked number. This was part of the problem. For years, I picked myself up off the floor, repairing the damage wreaked by Dan. I found a life I loved, carefree, with no responsibilities, just me savoring my waking moments. Yet with Theo, I reduced myself into a bottomless pit of need. Theo might be the jerk, but the problem was with me.

"Want to hang out after work?"

Over the last couple of weeks, the nighttime barrage of text messages had dwindled. The superhero community must have spread the word that I had narrowed my attention to one hero in particular. I stared at the message, decrypting its gay lingo. Why they didn't just come out and say, "Hey, want to get sweaty?" There was no doubt at this hour it was a request for a hookup.

A: Who is this?

S: Stretch. Hurt you didn't save my number.

It had been months since I served Stretch his Belgian ale. The man had the personality of cardboard, far stiffer than his superpowers suggested. He didn't exactly win in the conversation department, but I appreciated it when he came right out and asked if I wanted to spend the night on all fours. What self-respecting slut could say no to that offer?

Stretch's prowess in bed almost made up for the awkward pillow talk afterward. I couldn't have found my underwear fast enough. By the time I had my shoes on, he was talking about mutual funds and tax sheltering. Thankfully, he didn't expect the evening to be anything more than a transaction of pleasure. Anybody who says being able to elongate and thicken any part of your body at will is a stupid power. They obviously haven't been bent over the couch by them before.

A: What's up?

Did I really respond? What was I hoping to get out of this? It's not like I'd be sitting down with Stretch to discuss the path of destruction I left in my wake. Chances were, his text message had little to do with talking and more to do with my vigor on my knees.

S: Looking?

Gay men were odd creatures. They couldn't text a simple, "Want to fuck?" It had to either be cloaked in an activity that we all knew was code for sex. Then they'd swing to the other extreme, where sex turned into one-word discussions. I'm not saying I needed to be wooed every time I got naked. If you were going to pray to this altar, show a little respect.

A: For what?

S: You know.

A: Really? Coy isn't in my vocabulary.

Okay, that was a little harsh. But I wasn't in the mood to beat around the bush. I stared at the screen as the three dots appeared. What was I in the mood for? If the world crashed around me, then at least I could spend a night feeling good. Yes, what I wanted right now was a distraction to take my mind off the dumpster fire known as my love life.

S: I want to fuck you again.

Finally, to the point.

A: Where?

He texted his address, and I mapped the direction. I had forgotten he was only a couple of blocks from the club. Dan's voice pelted the back of my head with his searing words. He believed I was a player, willing to drop my pants for anybody who gave me the time of day. Then there was Theo, the one I wanted the time of day and couldn't get it. And with the club going away, long-term stability was almost laughable. In the immensity of Vanguard City, I had never felt so insignificant.

I wanted the voices to stop. The ache in my chest had reached a level that threatened to steal the air from my lungs. A panic attack hovered on the horizon. These feelings never crossed my mind when I lived in the moment. Perhaps it was the only direction in life for me? Making plans for the future hadn't panned out. It was time to return to my 'live for the moment' lifestyle.

Decision made.

A: omw.

The walk to Stretch's condo had been uneventful. No Eclipse sightings. No villains of any kind. The calm falling over the city meant the bad guys were sitting in their lairs holding planning sessions. At the rate they created groups to take out the heroes, they might as well form their own union. At least then they'd have dental.

The elevator doors closed, and I hesitated, pushing the button. The floor numbers had almost been worn beyond recognition. I studied my face on the silver surface. I wasn't at my best. Even as I forced a smile, I couldn't convince my eyes to lie. I was miserable, and it radiated outward.

"Just forget it, Al." Even the pep talk came across half-hearted. Stretch's mixture of absent personality, inability to carry a conversation, and outstanding performance in bed were the answer to all my problems. The Alejandro of the past was about to make a comeback.

I pushed the button for the seventh floor.

"Maybe he'll be naked and we can skip the small talk?"

With the way my luck had been going, I imagined he'd want to discuss politics. If I didn't fall asleep as he pontificated about the socio-economic status of Vanguard City and its need to invest in a sturdier infrastructure, maybe this wouldn't be so bad. Nope, my luck wasn't that good.

It was going to be subpar, three stars.

The doors slid open, and I gave my shoulders a quick shake. If nothing else, I'd walk away with another story for the breakfast table. I could already imagine Xander rolling his eyes, claiming most of my stories were fiction. Things would go back to normal, and right now, I needed that more than anything.

The hallways were dimly lit by sconces from the seventies, and I had to squint to read the door's numbers. The hallway smelled musty, despite the chemical lemon smell trying to hide it. When I reached Stretch's door, I went through the checklist. Breath? Not bad. Hair? Thoroughly tussled. Facial hair? Why did I care? He wouldn't appreciate the efforts.

I knocked.

The door opened into a dark room. I watched as Stretch's hand zipped through the entrance into the living room. I expected an awkward conversation and me pushing him to get naked. As I shut the door and followed his elastic limb, I found the room filled with candles and him in nothing but a mask and briefs.

"Looks like somebody got a head start."

"There was a charity event earlier. I put in a guest appearance to help them raise money. Did you know that in America, tall people have no workplace rights? Every day—"

Nope, I couldn't let him talk. "Glad you texted."

"Yeah, you know how charity work gets me hot and bothered."

I remembered why I hadn't responded to his messages the next day. Had my memory of him softened with time? If he continued, my memory wasn't the only thing that'd be staying soft.

I pulled at my tie. If we could fast forward through his definition of foreplay, we'd be at the fun stuff. Where his personality lacked, his other talents shined, or at least I hoped. I prayed I wasn't misremembering that as well.

"Why don't you have a seat?" He patted the spot on the couch next to him. Now we were heading in the right direction. Stretch usually maintained the typical superhero body, ripped with abs and pecs capable of crushing a soda can. But with me, he relaxed, showing a bit of the beer belly. Without his powers, I wondered what hid behind the elasticity.

I sat down next to the man. His arm snaked around the

side, stretching until he turned my head to face him. The lack of beard was disappointing. There was nothing I found sexier than a beard I could run my hands through, similar to how Theo...

I leaned in, kissing Stretch, jamming our lips together. He returned the kiss, his arm wrapping around my torso, squeezing me gently as his fingers grazed the front of my pants.

This was the second time that Eclipse had gotten into my head. I don't think it was his powers that had gotten under my skin. He dealt in fear and knew how to pull a single thread until I came completely undone. Just like before, I needed comfort and more than a little assurance. It had been the same thing that Theo...

I pulled back, shaking my head. My fingers touched my lips. I couldn't place my finger on the taste of Stretch's lips, but I knew it wasn't cinnamon.

My fingertips dug into my hand. I wanted to be angry that the burly man plagued my every thought. He had done something to me and I couldn't quite figure out what. The first time Eclipse used his powers, trying to drive me to suicide, it had been Theo who stood watch until the effects had vanished.

Stretch had yammered even though I barely listened. His fingers pulled at my zipper until he mentioned EO's name. I snapped back to reality, almost confused that the hero sitting on the couch wasn't the man in my daydreams.

"What did you say?"

"EO," he said. "I heard you and he were a thing now. I was surprised when you replied to my text."

Me too, hombre. Me, too.

Stretch wanted to get his rocks off. I couldn't blame him, but he would not watch over me as I worked through my demons. He wouldn't offer to leave the door open a crack. No, he wasn't the man I wanted right now, the man I *needed*.

"You want to move this to the bedroom?"

I stood up, and he promptly followed. "I need to go."

"Everything okay?"

His hand constricted, returning to a normal limb. I didn't know how to answer that question, not without having a breakdown in his living room.

"I'm a mess."

"Anything I can do to help?" For a moment, I thought he might be sincere. But as his hand reached for my zipper, I realized he'd say anything right now to get in my pants.

"I'm going to go."

"But—"

"I'm sorry."

I had made a terrible mistake. And in true Alejandro fashion, I doubled down and made even more. No, I needed to stop this train wreck before it got out of control. I turned around and headed for the door, zipping my pants as I went. I'm sure Stretch was confused. That made two of us. I'd owe him free drinks for life.

Right now, I didn't need to push away the pain I inflicted on myself. I needed to embrace it and figure out how I was going to move forward. A distraction wasn't what I needed. I needed a friend.

24

I WIPED AWAY THE TEARS. THEY HAD STARTED THE MOMENT I reached the street outside Stretch's condo. The taxi driver probably thought I was a hysterical mess. He wouldn't have been wrong. Forking over a twenty-dollar tip kept him from asking questions.

For the second time tonight, I found myself outside a man's apartment door. Closing my eyes, I inhaled through my nose. My lungs expanded, filling with scented carpet cleaner. The housekeeping staff did an outstanding job, leaving the common areas of the building immaculate. Exhaling through the mouth, I visualized the tension in my shoulders vanishing. I repeated it several times to make myself presentable. It wouldn't help the bloodshot eyes, but any victory tonight was worth noting.

I knocked on the door, a soft rap of the knuckles.

Waiting for a minute, I checked up and down the hall to make sure I didn't wake the neighbors. I repeated three soft taps. The deadbolt pulled back, and the door opened to bright light.

"Papi," I whispered.

Bernard couldn't respond before I pushed through the door, batting aside his hands. I wrapped my arms around his naked chest and buried my face. No amount of steadying breath prevented the next wave of tears. When his arms pulled me in tight, I lost it. The damn broke and I'm sure I broke into an ugly cry.

"Come inside."

With one arm, he lifted me as if I weighed nothing. He shut the door and carried me into his living room. Unlike Stretch, there were no attempts to grab at my groin or pull down my zipper. Right now, I needed somebody who'd lie to me and say everything would be okay. Bernard's chest would be wet in no time, but he made no move to pull away.

"¿Qué pasa, osito?"

Little bear. I didn't deserve his friendship. Eclipse had it wrong. I wasn't worried about Bernard turning his back on me. He was a hero, and he'd save anybody who needed it. The problem lay with me. Did I deserve to be saved? Or would I have been better off left beneath that building? My insecurities had steamrolled into questioning my self-worth. I knew better. I should stop. But right now, I fell into this pit and continued tumbling downward, waiting to hit the bottom.

Bernard didn't make it subtle as he carried me to the living room. Plopping me down on the couch, he took a seat on the ottoman. I hadn't been in his house for close to a year, but not a single thing was out of place. His artwork remained abstract, his personal items hidden from view. If I didn't know better, I'd say he was renting the apartment. It was one thing for the man to keep his thoughts to himself, but he didn't want his personality shining in his living space.

"Your taste in decorating is questionable." Yes, I deflected from the obvious issue. But how do you tell somebody your life is falling apart without it sounding dramatic? Especially when overdramatic was your default state.

"Gracias. I have excellent taste." Bernard's Spanish left something to be desired. His accent always sounded as if he were trying to imitate a character from a movie. But he knew the effort made me smile.

"Show me one thing in here that is you?"

"Are you avoiding the obvious?"

"Si."

"Do you want to talk about it?"

"One thing. Just one."

His sectional couch was large enough to entertain a decent-sized party, but he never invited us to his house. He had a long farm-style dining room table with eight chairs, but he didn't strike me as somebody who had dinner parties. I imagined if I went into his bedroom, it'd be a king-sized bed with his pillows off to one side. This bear was a conundrum. I filed it away for a future discussion.

"If you tell Griffin, I will incinerate you." He leaned over and opened the drawer at the edge of the couch. Pulling out a book, he dropped it in my lap. "I'll have Deathwalker bring you back to life, and then I'll kill you again."

A book? My eyes widened. Not just *any* book. He set a graphic novel on my lap. I recognized the character on the cover, the same bear sitting across from me. "You're reading a comic about yourself?"

"It's from a Centurions licensing deal. I like the artist. And..." Did Bernard's cheeks turn red? I had so many questions. "And you get to see what people think of you. It's like seeing your 'what if's' without having to deal with the results."

I flipped through the pages. Panel after panel, Sentinel struck heroic poses and hurled lighting at the bad guys. Sentinel always saved the day. It wasn't much different from reality.

"Dan showed up at the Alley."

The room flashed as Bernard's eyes crackled with energy. He blinked, shaking his head until his eyes returned to their soft brown. "Why?"

I started at the beginning. Every subtle detail, from the

meal with Theo all the way to Eclipse in the dress shop. The only time he broke his silence was when I revealed Eclipse as the leader of the Nocturnals. "I knew something was off about him. Continue." I even told him about Stretch and how I wound up in his apartment.

"Well..." He leaned forward, resting his elbows on his knees. His lips parted as if he might talk, and then he'd follow it up with a gesture and then froze. It was a lot to process, and in true Bernard fashion, he was for the most efficient way to explain himself. This is why it made total sense for him to be the public relations director for the Centurions.

"How do you feel about it?"

"All that Bernard wisdom, and that's what you come up with?"

"My opinions don't really matter, do they? It seems you're already grappling with outside..." he paused, choosing his words carefully. "Outside influences."

Eclipse, Dan, even Theo, so many voices pelting my brain. How did I feel about it? Theo hurt me. Dan attacked me, yet again. Eclipse, he just wanted to pick at a wound I thought long healed. The wound, the broken part of me, that was the source, the way each of these men had gotten under my skin.

"I'm scared." No humor, no avoidance. At the heart of it all, I was scared.

"Of?"

"What if Dan was right? What if *I* am the problem? What if—"

"Back it up, mister. That's about them. This is about you. You need to ignore them for a second and focus on Alejandro."

He rested a hand on my knee. From anybody else, it'd be dangerously close to the groin and get a rise out of me. However, as Bernard locked eyes with me, I could almost hear his thoughts. He was here. Present. He broke through those insecurities and reminded me I wasn't alone.

"What if I'm not good enough? Like, what if I don't deserve a happily ever after? I've built this life all about living in the moment. I love it; I really do. But..." I took a steadying breath. I should have known Bernard wouldn't let me wallow in my pity part. "I want a future I can look forward to."

"And you saw Theo in that future?"

"You know, I never wanted another relationship after Dan."

"My offer to kill him still stands."

I couldn't tell if he was joking. "Thanks, I think. But your whole hero thing, it might be a conflict of interest."

"I've saved enough lives. I've got hero karma. Besides, if a comet accidentally landed on his apartment, what would anybody say?"

It did not convince me he was joking. It was part of why I dragged my tired butt to breakfast every morning.

"Dan made it clear that I'd never be enough for anybody. I thought I'd be jealous of Theo's relationship with Julian. I mean, it's weird, right? But they're a cute couple. With Theo, I didn't need to be his everything."

"Do you want more?"

That was the million-dollar question. Did I want a man of my own? Somebody to throw down the label of "mine?" I didn't need to think about it, not even for a second. No. No, I didn't want to be somebody's everything. But I wanted to be somebody's something.

"I felt ignored."

"Did you tell him that?"

"I mean..." My face turned red. Had I assumed he possessed telepathy? No, I don't think so. He knew how I felt about ignoring my life-or-death text. But then he left. Did the two things have nothing in common? Had I—

"I overreacted."

"You're scared. This is new. It's different. It's weird, maybe wonderful, even. You're allowed to have all these feelings. But don't you think he'd want to hear this?"

"I hate when you're right."

"That must make me the most hated man in Vanguard."

"Bastardo. But Stretch..."

"You definitely make questionable choices." It stung coming from Bernard. "He has the personality of cardboard. I don't care how impressive he is in bed. You could have texted Maximus, or hell, that Golem guy. But you went with Stretch?"

"Are you mocking me?"

"Perhaps. I don't know EO, but you owe yourself a white flag. He put up with your antics so far."

"I'm charming, dammit."

Bernard lunged, arms wrapping around my chest. He squeezed me in a hug as he crawled on top of me. Being underneath a bearish superhero, I either had the best luck or maybe I had some decent friends. He let go, sitting next to me as he rubbed the back of my head. He strangled one of my insecurities, beating it to death with a little affection.

A storm brewed, emotions swirling about as I tried to sort through everything. But Bernard had given me a direction to walk, a safe route. It wasn't that simple. If I was going to make it to the other side, I needed to talk with Theo and put everything on the table. Vulnerability wasn't my strong suit.

"I'll grab a blanket and pillows. Make yourself comfortable, and you can fix your drama tomorrow."

Bernard got up, heading to the bedroom. He returned with a pile of linens and tossed them in my lap. I almost laughed at the sight of Sentinel striking poses on the sheets. He shot me a middle finger, coupled with a massive grin. Leave it to a friend to hold me upright when I couldn't do it for myself.

"Thanks for everything. I don't—"

"Deserve it? Shut your mouth, fool. You'd do the same if the tables were turned."

He vanished into his bedroom, leaving me with his superhero sheets. I hadn't thought I'd be sleeping with a superhero tonight after dashing out of Stretch's condo, but look at me. Even after Bernard's pep talk, the storm continued to swirl in the back of my head. I wouldn't get much sleep as I thought about that gash in my heart. First, I fix that, then I'd start repairing the rest of my life.

Tomorrow was going to be a long day.

25

At this hour, the city acted like a frantic ant farm on speed. People rushed from their homes to get to their jobs. With a cool breeze swirling through the streets, even those off-work milled about the streets. The HideOut would be packed this morning, and if Chad hadn't saved our usual table, there'd be hell to pay.

Without fail, in the dead of night, superheroes were called to save the world. I woke to an empty apartment and a note from Bernard promising to meet me for breakfast. I had to wonder if being able to share his secret with somebody was a weight off his chest or if he worried I'd spill the beans. Anybody who claimed I couldn't keep a secret... okay, they probably knew I was a blabbermouth.

"Griffin is going to be so pissed that I found out first." Childish, I know. But when it came to this member of our breakfast squad, having the scoop on superhero antics could be traded like currency. I'm sure he'd eventually learn about Theo's identity. It was the price of dating an average person. Secret identities weren't as guarded as they used to be. Only the A-listers, like the Centurions, needed to hide their alter-egos, or they'd be hunted like vermin around the clock.

Chad had removed some of the plywood from one window, making it feel like the coffee shop had luxurious outdoor views. When your business got wrecked as frequently as they did in the Ward, you learned to take lemons and make lemonade. I pushed opened the door to the HideOut, and the bells jingled overhead. I froze, confused at the sight in front of me. Not only were two people sitting at *our* table, but they had also taken my seat.

"Scarlet?"

Chad stood up, waving me over. Something in the world was not right. My life between the HideOut and Midnight Alley never converged. I liked it that way. To see my soon-to-be ex-boss and my favorite barista mingling could only spell disaster. I approached with caution. This could, in fact, be the start of the apocalypse.

"Why have you never introduced us? She is an absolute delight."

"Yeah..." I pulled out Bernard's usual chair and took a seat. "She is. At work."

"Alejandro," she laughed as she held up her coffee cup in a salute. "Dear, I'm a delight no matter where I am."

"All I get to hear about is the next morning. Alejandro drags his tired butt in here from who knows where."

"Oh," she laughed, "I know where. I see the men he leaves with."

"Do all heroes wear cheap cologne?" Chad asked.

They both stared at me as if it wasn't a rhetorical question. I didn't like this, not one bit. These two should never be allowed to compare notes about my life. If ever I needed a supervillain to ruin my day, it was now. Bring on the worst the universe offered.

"He *does* have a type."

"I don't like this. You two aren't allowed to be friends. Chad, don't you have coffee to make?"

"I think the kids are managing the kitchen just—"

"Chad," I barked. "Coffee."

"Is he this pushy at work? You might need to meet with Human Resources."

Chad reluctantly stood. I could almost hear him weighing the need to make a dollar and the gossip about to be dished. He was a great guy, but I'm convinced he'd sell the coffee shop if I had a tasty enough morsel. He shot me a look before moving behind the counter.

"Chad was just telling me you have some pretty, dare I say, impressive, stories for breakfast. I have seen the wrath of your charm at the bar, but I never get to hear the aftermath. There's a joke in there about taking the tip."

My jaw dropped.

"Don't pretend you maintain any semblance of purity. You're a scoundrel, and thank God you're *my* scoundrel."

"I'll have you know. There's plenty that is pure about me."

"Pure bullshit, perhaps." She raised an eyebrow while she sipped her coffee. Scarlet would get along with the guys. Her mix of witty jabs and honesty would be well received. I was betting, with enough caffeine coursing through her veins, she'd spill a tale or two of her own.

"I'm always happy to see you, but—"

"Why are you seeing me with the sun up?"

"It's bright enough I can see your crow's feet."

"You're fired." She let out a long sigh. "Huh. I forgot how delightful it is to terminate an employee. I wish I had done that more often."

"You couldn't fire me if you—"

"Read my lips, Alejandro." Scarlet's face no longer carried hints of joy. Her eyes hardened and I'm certain her jaw tightened. "You're. Fired." And as if it meant nothing, she took another sip.

"Scarlet. I... uh..." It was bad enough my employment had a doomsday clock hanging overhead. But to be fired before she sold the club? I was about to scream about the world conspiring against me. After giving her years of loyal service, how could she—

She slapped her hand down on the table, snapping me out of my downward spiral. Something clacked against the tabletop. When she pulled away her hand, she revealed a silver ring with two keys. I couldn't imagine what she was trying to tell me. I picked them up, examining the ring as if it might be something other than the obvious.

"Thanks, I think?"

"I can't have you working as a bartender if you're going to take over as the general manager."

"Oh, a promotion." Chad slid a cup of coffee in front of me. His ability to appear for the juicy bits no longer bordered on supernatural. I was going to add him to the HeroApp™. The Gossiper, knower of all dirty secrets. "Congratulations. Coffee is on the house." And as fast as he appeared, he zipped off toward his other patrons.

"Why bother promoting me? Can't exactly manage a boarded-up nightclub."

Scarlet leaned back in her chair. With a slow and steady motion, she folded a leg over her knee. It had been years since she worked as a hero, but the fluid motion made it clear she had complete mastery of her body. I bet she spent more than a couple of hours at the gym each week. Her beauty wasn't even close to the most alluring part of her being.

"Funny you should say that."

I leaned forward, waiting for the follow-up. She let the silence hang in the air. I couldn't handle her theatrics. I was already a nerve rubbed raw.

"Spit it out, woman."

"Eclipse made me an offer, a very generous one. He—"

"He's a supervillain, by the way."

"Oh, I know. When he first made his offer, I did some research. Once I started digging, I found he has more than a few ties to the villains in the city. After that, the union asked me to keep him occupied."

"You were working him over?"

"You're not the only one who knows how to grab a man's attention." The smirk and waggle of the eyebrows made me laugh. Scarlet was indeed a vixen. "But he wasn't getting his hands on my baby. Sorry I couldn't tell you sooner."

"So you're staying? Stepping down? Scarlet, you're killing me."

"A buyer approached me."

I ran down the list of heroes who had enough money to buy the club. The general population thought that heroes were all rich and living in their penthouses. Most of them had regular day jobs and treated heroing as a hobby. Saving the city didn't come with a paycheck. And the few heroes with rich alter-egos, I couldn't imagine Scarlet handing over her years of hard work to them.

"They had one demand." She eyed the keys. "They'd

purchase the club as long as you agreed to take over as the manager."

"I— I— " I stared at the keys. Scarlet had said she wished I could buy the club. I had put the outlandish statement out of my mind. I worked for tips, and putting money away in the bank wasn't high on my priority list. Even if she had been willing to sell it for a buck, I'd have to check my balance.

"Say yes, you idiot."

"Do what she said, you idiot." Thanks, Chad, your words of encouragement were helpful.

"I don't know. That's..." I had told Bernard I wanted to plan for the future. Somewhere, there was a happy middle ground. Taking over as the manager would mean more responsibility, but there's no place I'd rather spend my nights. It'd give me access to a future that currently felt just out of reach.

"Scarlet, I need your brutal honesty." It was a hard question to ask. I needed to hear somebody say it. "Do you think I can handle it?"

She didn't hesitate with a loud laugh. It came from the stomach, and a second later, everybody in the cafe was giggling like they had heard the funniest joke. Even I chuckled, amused at Scarlet's powers washing across the shop.

"Mi amigo, there is nobody I have more faith in. You

have proven to be resilient, creative, and feisty. Midnight Alley will thrive with you at the helm."

I had surrounded myself with wonderful people. When my confidence plummeted and left me flailing, they'd be there to pick me up. Ironic that this breakfast table should be the nexus of where those friends gathered.

"I'll do it." And just like that, a world of possibilities rolled out before me.

"Congratulations! The other business owners will give you a hand." Yes, even Chad made the cut. He gave me a bump with his hip as I fought to keep my face from turning bright red.

"Stonewall will be thrilled."

"Wait. What? Back that up."

"Oh," she laughed, "did I forget to mention your boyfriend's husband bought the club? Technically, both of them did."

It was like being beneath the building again. A wall of bricks came slamming down and my brain refused to process what she said. They did what? How? Why?

"We have drawn up the paperwork. All it needs is my signature."

"They bought the club..." I was mumbling.

"You, as the manager, was the only stipulation. Our lawyers spent more time arguing over who got to tell you. But let's be honest, I get what I want, and here we are."

Julian and Theo had bought the club? But more than

that, these married heroes wanted me to spearhead the Alley's next iteration. Had this been before I texted Theo to break off our relationship?

"It was cute how much they wanted to keep it a secret. Glad to see they pulled it off."

While I let my insecurities consume me, Theo was taking his status as a hero to a new level. Was this why he had been distant? Had I read the situation wrong? I had made a horrible mistake.

But as every electronic device in the cafe buzzed to life, I didn't have time to focus on my stupidity. I fished around in my pocket for my phone. There were multiple dots on the HeroApp™ map. It had been a while since the villains had coordinated their efforts. Things were about to get crazy.

I showed Scarlet my screen. "The city's under attack."

26

"The Nocturnals," Scarlet hissed.

"Eclipse," I said. When she raised her eyebrow, I realized that her research hadn't filled in the complete puzzle. "He's the leader of the Nocturnals. See, I do my research too."

Her eyes went wide as the pieces fell into place. "Should have been obvious with the white suits. Villains these days are so lazy." The HeroApp™ vibrated again, a black dot somewhere on the block. The HideOut had recovered from the last attack. How did businesses survive being blown up repeatedly? I should find out if I was going to be running the Alley.

While the rest of the coffee shop held their breath, she jumped to her feet. Stiletto heels flew across the cafe as she stormed to the door. If that didn't signify she meant business, she tore a slit up the side of her dress. I realized she was going into a firefight without backup.

"You can't go out there." Yup, she ignored me.

"Damn," Chad said. "A lady hasn't had me this hot and bothered since—"

"Call Bernard. Tell him to get the Centurions," I shouted at Chad. I ran through the door to see her standing in the middle of the street. I had never seen her in action, and standing there alone, she almost seemed petite. It had been years since she wore a cape. I didn't expect a retired hero to—

Scarlet spun about, dropping low with her fist balled. The uppercut struck a white blur under the chin, sending a massive man soaring twenty feet into the air. She landed on one knee, the pavement cracking under her weight.

"Was the superhero pose necessary?" I mumbled.

The man spun head over feet before he regrouped. He came flying toward her, this time a fist posed to drive her beneath the city street. Scarlet hummed, her hair lifting from her shoulders. My jaw dropped as the woman hovered off the ground. My boss, no, my former boss, had come out of retirement for a one-night performance.

"Kick his ass," I yelled.

"You have no superpowers." The words were lyrical, as if stolen from a song on the radio. The power rolled along my skin, causing the hair to stand on end. If I had superpowers, I'd be questioning them right now. She had chosen her words carefully.

The man fell out of the air, skidding along the pavement until he came to a stop only a few feet away. The phone vibrated and more black blips appeared. This wasn't a haphazard attempt at terror. The Nocturnals coordinated their efforts. But they weren't the only ones.

"Mind if we have this dance?" Hyperion landed next to Scarlet before she fell back to her feet. The Ward's heroes had never been territorial, but I was glad to see them step in. Scarlet could handle one of Eclipse's flunkies, but could she withstand their combined might?

A man appeared behind her, knocking her into a nearby building. Before Hyperion could respond, the villain grew the size of a building and attempted to squash the hero with the heel of his foot. Hyperion fell to his knees, holding his hands up, an invisible barrier keeping the newest foe from flattening him.

In the blink of an eye, he vanished as the asphalt broke apart. My nerves weren't made for this. I was about to squeal—

"Ouch, that could have hurt," Hyperion said. I turned to see the man hovering next to me. The Zipper gave me a wave. I let out a sigh, thankful the speedster had saved the day.

"They're everywhere," I said, as if they didn't already know that. I was about to launch into how Scarlet had clobbered the unconscious guy. But neither of them was anywhere to be found. "Wait, where's Scarlet?"

"She's at the hospital," Zipper said. "Him, on the other hand..."

Thunder roared through the city despite there being no clouds. Lightning hammered into the chest of the giant, the source somewhere above the Ward. I didn't know the name of every hero like Griffin or how to stop them from dying like Xander. But even I could identify the titan flying into view. The Nocturnals should run. Papi had arrived to spank the bad guys.

Hyperion shot into the air, and Zipper vanished before I could chuckle at my bad joke. Now that Scarlet had been taken to safety, it was time for me to get back in the coffee shop and shelter underneath a sturdy table. The Centurions had arrived and, like always, they'd mop the floor with the bad guys. Bernard best give Eclipse an extra punch to the mouth for me.

With a step backward, I moved from the street to the sidewalk. I did one last sweep to see if Theo or Julian had arrived to help the local heroes. I didn't want Theo in harm's way, but I would have paid money to see one of his portals opening for the cavalry to arrive and save the day.

"What are you up to, Eclipse?" I swear, it was barely a whisper. But somehow the universe heard. I watched the smoke roll from behind me through my legs. I should have known better than to ask a stupid question. And to say it out loud? I invited disaster. I'd be mocked later for not listening to Señor Kendrick in the fifth grade.

I spun about, lobbing a fist. My knuckles vanished into the smoke and struck something hard as granite. I refused to scream in front of the villain, but I was pretty sure I had broken a finger or two. My deadliest weapon was a scathing commentary. I should have stuck with what I know.

"I'm getting the impression you're stalking me. If you wanted—"

The hand shot out of the smoke, a white glove and white sleeves. His fingers wrapped around my throat, and there was no point in flailing. If Eclipse wanted to kill me, it'd have happened already. No, just like every other egomaniac, he had a grudge. I'm sure before long, he'd be explaining his master plan and by the time he finished, half the heroes of Vanguard would be lined up to kick his ass.

"They'll save me." Right? My life couldn't end, not now. I had unfinished business before I let this jerk kill me.

"They'll try." Eclipse stepped out of the smoke. The hood and suit looked different from the ones he wore at the club, but it was the same guy. If self-entitlement had a cologne, it'd be whatever he had bathed himself in before going on a villainous bender.

"What do you want..." Okay, breathing was getting difficult. I'd appreciate any of the thousand heroes in the city to arrive. They'd have a pithy exchange and then fists would fly. "... want with me?"

Eclipse laughed. Even his genuine, amused laugh that started in the pit of his stomach came with arrogance. His hand tightened and, without so much as a grunt, he lifted me into the air. I attempted a kick to his leg. I'm pretty sure I hurt myself more than him.

"You thought this was about you? You sad fool. This was never about a mediocre bartender. You were just an amusing addition."

The world dimmed. Either his smoke had gotten thicker, or I was about to pass out from the lack of oxygen. Neither of them sounded like a fun way to end my morning. Eclipse leaned in, his cheek brushing mine. If he kissed me, I would not be happy. I didn't need it to be any weirder than it was.

"It's the heroes I'm after."

I closed my eyes as my limbs jerked involuntarily. My lungs burned, but there was no air. I was about to die, and the last thing I'd have seen was this ugly bastard.

"They'll burn. Each and every one."

27

Something tugged at the hair on my wrists. I tried pulling away, but he had tied something around my hands. They were trapped behind my back, and I— I was alive. I laid on a cold surface, bound but alive. Before I opened my eyes, I ran through my senses. Body hurt. No real sound other than the whizzing of fans. It smelled as if it might rain, but that would not save the day. I skipped sticking my tongue out to taste the dread of the situation.

I opened my eyes. Wherever Eclipse had taken me, it was about as far from the city street as imaginable. The room was circular, filled with wall-to-wall computer screens and, in the middle, a massive round table. On the far wall, windows looked out into the sky. We were up high, perhaps in a skyscraper in Vanguard? Whatever this place was, it had a familiarity to it, as if I had spent time here as a kid.

Rolling over, I found Eclipse pawing at a computer terminal. I could hear his growling over the clicking and beeping of the equipment. I assumed his secret lair would be underground, perhaps a sewer. No, no, not with that white suit. He probably hid at a dry cleaner as he plotted to —I had no idea what his goals might be.

Then I saw the seven tubes, each with a mannequin inside.

Getting up to my knees, I could make out the sigil on the table, the official logo of the Centurions. That fool had all but invited a superhero battle from the world's most victorious team. Why here? No matter how powerful he believed himself to be, this was a battle he couldn't win. Eclipse did a lot of questionable things, but putting himself in jeopardy was not one of them.

"Thanks," I said, shambling to my feet.

"You're awake. I thought you were going to miss the best part of the day."

"Oh, no. I'll be awake when the Centurions kick your ass."

He laughed. "Obviously, you missed the genius of our plan."

I prepared to spit back a retort, but froze. I knew the Centurions had a large staff. Beneath this floor were operations, public relations, and even an auditorium where

Centurions talked to their fans. But after the documentary, *The 99th Floor* aired, the entire world knew this space was off-limits to anybody but the Centurions themselves. Unless one of the heroes returned, Eclipse could go about his machinations undisturbed.

"They're busy with the rest of the Nocturnals. We've been systematically targeting the Centurion's allies. Vanguard's top heroes are difficult to mobilize unless you're a giant fire-breathing lizard threatening the White House. But we managed."

"Decoys?"

"You're not just a pretty face."

"So you've broken into the 99th floor? What now? What's your endgame, Eclipse?"

"My employer wants the Centurions nullified."

How much information could I get? When I saw Bernard again, I'd be able to pass it all along. Perhaps some tidbit would tip the scales and they'd wipe the floor with this mysterious boss.

"Is that why you wanted the club? For your boss?"

Eclipse turned, the growling turning into a snarl. Good to know it struck a nerve.

"So many heroes in one place. We could have crippled the heroes of Vanguard by removing them one at a time. He didn't see the genius of the plan." Eclipse threw his hands up in the air. "There are more heroes than the Centurions. But look who I'm telling. You *know* most of them."

I ignored the slut shaming. "Too bad Scarlet didn't fall for it. Stonewall and EO ruined that plan."

"Don't worry, I'll be taking care of them as well. I can't have loose threads getting in the way."

The binding on my back made it impossible for me to reach for my phone. I swear, if I got out of here, I'd lose a few pounds. Maybe this would be what prompted me to pick up that old gym membership. I just needed to make it out alive.

"Looking for this?" Eclipse held up my phone.

"Hey. Give that back."

"Soon as I finish here."

"Password?"

"Your mom's birthday." Not my best retort, but I was running on steam. I knew it'd be my mouth that got me in trouble one day. Eclipse barreled toward me, moving faster than should be possible. The day had come. My mouth was going to get me killed.

"It's beyond me what he sees in you. You must be dynamite in the sack." He grabbed my shirt, dragging me close enough that I could smell his breath through the mask. He thought poking at my insecurities would do more damage than a punch. Eclipse obviously didn't understand how much I had already beat myself up. If I had been smart, I'd have kept my mouth shut.

"I'd have ruined you," I shouted. "You'll never find out what you're missing." He could have struck me down or hurled me across the Centurion's base. I prepared myself for a world of pain, so much that I flinched as he pushed the phone in my face. If he wanted dick pics, he just needed to ask.

"You are only a means to an end. I couldn't care less if you died. Mundanes aren't worth my efforts."

"Your mom—"

Now, he threw me. The glass monitor shattered under my weight. I went limp like they taught us in school. It did nothing to stop the pain in my back. I landed on the floor, the wind knocked from my lungs, and all I could focus on was my inability to draw air. Glass cracked under me. I couldn't stop, not now. Whatever he was about to—

"Burn. You blocked his number? Is there trouble in paradise?"

Shit. He unlocked my phone so he could make a phone call. I prayed Theo was saving the world. I didn't want him to respond, not today. Let one of the Centurions come and save me. I wanted Theo and Julian as far from this lunatic as possible.

He raised the phone to his ear and waited for Theo to answer. "Oh, I'm sorry. Alejandro is busy bleeding on the floor."

I could only draw the tiniest of breaths, but I forced myself onto my stomach. Dragging along the glass, I ignored the pain pulsing down my ribs and into my tail-bone. I opened my mouth to warn Theo, to tell him not to come, but nothing came out of my mouth. I failed him. Eclipse would lead him into danger, and there wasn't a thing I could do to stop the villain.

"That's a lot of vulgarity from a hero." Eclipse took pleasure in the misery of others. His powers were only fitting. "I'm not sure how much longer I can resist breaking his smug jaw. You should hurry. Tootles."

That arrogant asshole. It had never been about me. He wanted to use me as bait. He threw the phone in my direction as he waltzed toward the screens. The maniacal laugh might have been cliche, but something on the monitor elicited a terrifying chuckle.

"I've won. Do you hear me? I've already won."

The certainty in his voice offered no room for debate. What had this villain done? At least he was too occupied with his own genius to notice I discovered a piece of the screen to slice my way through my restraints. What was I going to do once I was free? I'd figure it out as I went. Theo and Julian were about to walk into a trap. If I could get to my phone, I'd be able to warn them.

The movies made getting free look easy. If I sawed any harder, the glass would slice through my hands. Maybe once I joined the gym to firm up that belly, I'd take one of their "Escape the Villain" classes for adults. With the number of times I got kidnapped, I could probably teach a master's course on what not to do.

Free. I glanced down at my hands and fought the urge

to hurl. Blood. More blood than I hoped for. The jerk had used duct tape to keep me locked up. Now to see if I could reach the phone before he did one of those super blitzes and knocked me across the room again.

Theo needed me. Julian needed me. Hell, the Centurions needed me. I was their last defense before Eclipse enacted whatever diabolical plan he had up his sleeve.

It was five, maybe six feet. I just needed to get my feet under me and sprint. My superpower was the lightning speed at which I could send a text message. Not even Zipper could compete. I just needed to—

I pushed off, running. The surrounding glass cracked as I almost slipped. Four feet. My lungs refused to cooperate. I'd send the message and pass out after. Two feet. I reached out as Eclipse turned around, his crazed laughter stopping. Phone. We had a co-dependent relationship. Even as it pressed against the cuts, it snuggled against my palm.

Unlock. I punched the keys. Trap.

Eclipse barreled into me. The room spun about as I flew across the Centurion's base.

"Oomph." I smacked the floor with a thud, the phone sliding out of my hands. I reached, trying to crawl toward the device. But the world was turning fuzzy as my lungs decided they had had enough. It was time to admit defeat. I wasn't a hero, and there was no way I could defeat Eclipse. He stood over me, placing a foot on my chest.

"You tire me. I hoped you'd get to see me crush your

men. But it looks like you're going to die alone." His foot pushed down on my ribs, threatening to break my sternum. Behind the mask, I imagined he smiled, satisfied with his handiwork.

But it was my turn to smile.

"I'm not alone."

28

THE PORTAL OPENED TO ECLIPSE'S SIDE. IT MIGHT BE THEO'S doing, but it was Julian who came flying out. He wrapped Eclipse in a bear hug, tackling him with a deafening roar. I coughed, causing a bolt of pain down my body as the sound of fists pounding meat filled the base.

Julian was a bruiser, stronger than the average hero. But it didn't seem to slow Eclipse. They rolled about on the ground, Julian landing a punch to the face and Eclipse returning the favor. Neither slowed as the other continued their hammering.

In a puff of smoke, Eclipse shot backward, landing on his feet, squaring up for another round of slugging. Julian got to his feet as Eclipse hovered in a thick covering of black smoke. If it had just been about strength, I believed Julian would wipe the floor with this half-baked villain.

But Eclipse had powers beyond strength, and if they affected others as much as they did me, Julian was in danger.

With a thunderous clap from his hands, the smoke around Eclipse dissipated, leaving him in his bright cape flapping in the wind. Julian charged, but seconds before driving his shoulder into Eclipse, he vanished through a portal.

"Theo," I whispered.

Eclipse turned, looking for his opponent. Theo predicted his movements, or maybe he was watching through a portal somewhere in the Centurion's base. But as the void opened behind Eclipse, Julian flew out fast enough that his fists hammered Eclipse in the back. Good, I hope he snapped the man in half.

Eclipse soared across the room, slamming into the support holding a bank of windows in place. Half the windows in the Centurion's base exploded, raining shards of glass on the streets below. A few inches in either direction and Eclipse would fall to his doom. I never wished for a person to die, but this asshole came close. I didn't want him to die, but hurt? Yes, I wanted him to hurt a lot.

"I wasn't sure you'd come to save your plaything."

"Is somebody jealous Alejandro wouldn't touch his peepee?"

It wasn't the statement that made me grin. It bordered on comical as he winked in my direction. He made a show of it so Eclipse wouldn't miss the gesture. If my ribs didn't feel like smashed twigs, I'd have laughed.

"That's *my* man you're talking about."

Theo fell from a portal directly above Eclipse. He balled his fists together, slamming them down on Eclipse's head. Eclipse swatted at him, sending him barreling through the air. I nearly cried out for him when he vanished into another portal.

"You're going to pay for touching him." Julian's words weren't a threat. As he clenched his fists, I could see the promise written on his face. Whatever insecurity I had been feeling wavered as these two men fought a villain. For me. They fought for *me*.

A portal opened outside the building, behind Eclipse. Theo flew out like Julian had, knocking Eclipse forward. The villain vanished into a portal and reappeared in front of Julian, just in time to receive an uppercut, launching him twenty feet upward into the ceiling.

They fought like a well-oiled machine. They were heroes, and more than that, they were partners. I had been jealous that I'd never be able to compete with their bond. They had invited me into their lives, a romance and a friendship. Now they fought to save the city. To save me.

I felt foolish. It rattled my insides almost as much as Eclipse had when he smacked me. But as they coordinated their attack, both of them continued glancing in my direction. They might not be able to kneel by my side to ensure I was okay, but they were doing what they could. The parallels between their rescue and my relationship with Theo were not lost on me.

Eclipse fell, leaving a perfect impression of himself in the ceiling. Before he landed in Julian's outstretched arms, he blitzed away in a puff of smoke, and reappeared only a few feet from me, the smoke rolling over me. I scurried away, not wanting a repeat of the last time he used his powers on me. The pain didn't matter. Anything to avoid another trip through the alternate realities in my imagination.

"His powers," I shouted. "He uses your fears."

Both Theo and Julian remained frozen. Eclipse's smoke wrapped around their legs, crawling up their bodies. He had them trapped, drowning in their shortcomings. I prayed these heroes had confronted their fears and that they'd be able to break free. Then they could throw Eclipse out the window once and for all.

"Oh, this is good," Eclipse hissed. "It appears your heroes are nothing more than bravado and muscle. I can taste the fear they pretend doesn't exist. They're even weaker than you."

Eclipse staggered to his feet as the black smoke wrapped around him like a blanket. With a step in my direction, he almost stumbled. They had been so close to beating him, to ending his terrorizing of Vanguard. More smug laughter between spits of coughing. As he raised his hand, pointing at me, there was nothing I could do. I was helpless.

I screamed as the tendril of black drilled into my forehead.

Just like before, it started in the darkness. I could hear Eclipse's obnoxious laughter in the background. It was the same image of Theo and Julian jesting about my insignificance. Unlike the villain's previous attempts, I came armed.

His powers put me in the restaurant again, determined to pull at my weakest moment. I was staring at a mirror version of myself. I was about to reach for the phone and confirm my misconstrued perception of the situation. Eclipse thought he had won, that he was about to turn me into a teary-eyed mess.

Theo apologized for the missed text message. I accepted it, an honest mistake. Eclipse would need to do more than repeat the same tricks if he wanted my attention.

"Not this time."

I had fought off his abilities when he'd tried to use Bernard against me. It wasn't logic that combatted his abilities. Somewhere in my chest, in my heart, I knew Eclipse was wrong. His powers could tug at my fears, but they wouldn't wreak havoc like before. With a little help from the men in my life, I faced my fears, and I was prepared for battle.

"No," I whispered.

The image of the restaurant shook like an earthquake shock wave tore at the ground under our feet. For our third tussle, I'd be the winner. I had to. Theo had watched over me the first time it happened. It was time to return the favor.

"No," I screamed.

My mirror-self reached for the phone. As the text message came in, I picked up the phone to see a message from Julian. I thought he had butted in *our* moment. But the image shifted to Julian in a suit, meeting with a man in a suit of metal armor. I recognized the Machinist from the HeroApp™, but had no idea how he played into Eclipse's theatrics.

"You and Theo are sure? Once you sign, the club is good as yours."

Julian nodded before checking his phone. He punched at it furiously, ending with the swoosh as the message was sent.

"What do you know about running a club?"

"I don't. Alejandro Martinez, however, he'll continue Midnight Alley's legacy."

"The bartender?" The Machinist raised an eyebrow before nodding in agreement. "He makes a killer cocktail."

This wasn't my memory. Was Eclipse pulling at my

imagination? I had never thought about what happened on the other side of that call. No, this wasn't my memory at all. Whatever that villain was doing, he had unwittingly given me access to missing puzzle pieces. Did he think we'd be too busy with our own suffering to steal a glance into each other's heads?

"Are you sure?"

I spun about to see Julian and Theo curled together in bed. I recognized the coat of glistening sweat. Had it been earlier in the day, the sight of them together might have tugged at my jealousy, but Eclipse continued to miss his mark.

"Whether or not you ask him out, I'm going to invite him out for drinks."

Julian had wrapped himself around Theo. His enormous frame dwarfed his partner. As Julian kissed the back of the little man's neck, it reminded me of how Theo spooned against my back.

"I think I'm going to ask him out." Theo rolled over, cupping Julian's face, giving him a kiss passionate enough that I blushed. The big lug might not be my type, but there was something beautiful about seeing two men intertwined. Not to mention it was hot, so damned hot.

"You're nervous!" Julian exclaimed.

"You should have seen him with the Naga. He barely batted an eyelash. Are you sure asking out a guy I rescued is a good idea?"

Julian patted him on the chest. "You owe him an apology for leaving him on the roof. It's the least you could do."

This wasn't my memory either. Did Eclipse think that showing me this would shake my faith in what Theo and I shared? Was this intentional, or did he not understand that a person was capable of feelings other than jealousy and rage?

"Okay, let's go." Julian kicked off the sheets. "Get dressed. We're going to the club."

Theo's eyes were wide in disbelief. It was more endearing than I could have imagined. As Theo reached for the cock, the sweet moment turned naughty. The big man froze. Wow! We'd need to discuss the size of that later. *Everything* about Julian was big.

"Right after I finish this."

I could feel the heat rise in my cheeks and my pants. Even in the face of danger, my lil' sidekick wanted attention.

The image faded away just as it was getting interesting. In the distance, standing in a pair of spotlights, Theo and Julian appeared to be sleeping while upright. I didn't know how to shake them from Eclipse's powers. I might be able to fight my battle... Could I walk into their minds? Could they see my thoughts?

Mentalists. Their powers were annoying as hell. I could

throw a punch, but fighting on the psychic plane was like driving blindfolded after one too many martinis.

"Let..." The growl came from my gut. "Me..." I unleashed a howl. "Out."

The darkness broke.

Centurion headquarters. It was a mess, with broken monitors, twisted beams, and glass scattered across the floor. I hoped this didn't come out of Bernard's paycheck. I almost felt bad for Papi.

Eclipse stood in a cloud of smoke, almost as still as Theo and Julian. Whatever he was doing to the two men, it required his attention. Both of them were whimpering, small sounds that bordered on sobs. I had been the victim of Eclipse twice. I knew whatever they were feeling was going to take days to shake off. But for now, I needed their help with beating the bad guy.

Alejandro, the hero of heroes. I imagined the reporter citing me as the savior of the city as I climbed to my feet. Maybe they'd build a statue in my honor. It'd replace the Centurion's monument. It'd be the least they could do for saving their base of operations. Alejandro Day, a citywide holiday. Yup, I'd be talking to Bernard about making it a reality.

I charged. My lungs hurt, my ribcage ached, and my

spine screamed in agony. Eclipse should have known better than to turn his back on the non-powered guy. He'd learn his lesson.

"No," I shouted, "capes."

Grabbing the flapping white piece of fabric, I wrapped it around his neck. I grabbed the sides, pulling it back, bracing my knee in the middle of his back. My muscles strained as I yanked as hard as I could. I wanted to choke the villain. If I couldn't breathe, I wanted him to experience the same.

His body stiffened. He was no longer occupied by Theo and Julian as he swung about, trying to shake me. Both knees pushed into his back. The blood on my hands left streaks of red on his costume. My grip was slipping, but I was determined to stop the asshole from winning. Riding him like a bucking bronco, I refused to relent.

"Just die," I yelled.

He reached behind his head, trying to grab at my face. When he couldn't reach me, he found my wrist. I prepared for another ascent across the room. But this time he pulled me off, sneering as he held me off the ground, dangling like a rag doll.

"Better luck next time," he coughed. I managed a cough. Not the victory I—

Eclipse spun, hurling me across the room and out the window of the 99th floor. I'd have a few seconds to ponder my existence as I plummeted a thousand feet to my demise.

Adrenaline coursed through my veins, my thoughts trying to focus on anything but the pavement rushing toward my face.

"No!" Not far behind me, Julian barreled out of the window, Eclipse captured in a bear hug. The bruiser kicked Eclipse away, narrowing his body until he was gaining speed and closing the gap between us. Even if he reached me, even if he could wrap himself around me, we'd hit the ground like a bomb.

"Got you." Even shouting, the words were barely audible over the gushing wind. Julian pulled at my leg, positioning my back against his chest. He spun around, so he'd act as a cushion between me and the street below. He might be strong, but there was no way he'd survive the impact. Could he?

At least I had the perfect view of Eclipse flailing as he fell. The puffs of smoke appeared, but he seemed unable to zip away like before. Good, if I was going to wind up a smear on the street, I wanted his matching stain nearby. Was he convinced he had won now? I almost laughed, a wave of pain pulsing through my chest.

"Thanks for trying, Julian." He couldn't hear me, but I couldn't die without acknowledging the hero attempting to save me.

I watched the sign on the front of the building fly past. That meant only a few more floors until we—

Suddenly we changed directions, flying upward above

the city. Our momentum carried us far above the 99th floor. From here, I could see the entire skyline of Vanguard City. It was beautiful, but I couldn't admire it as I tried to figure out how we went from falling to soaring. Could Julian fly?

Then I saw the portal. It wasn't one hero saving me. I nearly forgot that I was in league with a dynamic duo.

Our ascent slowed, the momentum fading. Why had Theo teleported us higher than before? Was he testing my constitution? First, I'd kiss him, then I'd hit him. No, switch the order.

As we started our descent, a portal opened beneath us. Six feet below, Julian landed with a thud, arms wrapped around me. Theo gasped as he held his hands out to his side, glowing with purple energy.

"Next time, give me a chance to catch my breath."

He collapsed to his knees and the portal closed. Julian let go, and I rushed to Theo as fast as my tired body allowed. I wrapped my arms around him before Julian's arms covered us both. I ignored the pain, focusing on the warmth of his suit pressed against my face. His breathing was quick and shallow, but he was okay.

"Got your text," he said between gasps.

"Are you okay?"

"Five-by-five. Just need to catch my breath." He patted me on the cheek, putting his forehead against mine. "Thanks for the assist."

"I told him his suit was dumb. He should have listened."

It was Julian's turn to laugh. "Do you think he got away?" The big man got up, heading to the window.

"They always get away," I said. "I'm not taking that bet."

"Well," Julian said, looking out the window. "I take no pride in this, but you owe me money."

"Really?" asked Theo.

"That's going to be a lot of paperwork."

The solemn tone of Julian's quip surprised me. I don't know why I thought they'd be high-fiving over the victory. Heroes wanted to save more than the victim. My respect for their job continued to grow.

"His powers," Theo said, "are hellish. How'd you break free?"

"I was already living my worst fear." He pulled away, an eyebrow raised. Just say it Alejandro, don't be an idiot. If this was going to work, I needed to be honest with him, Julian, and myself.

"The thought of losing you, both of you. It doesn't get much worse than that."

Theo pulled me closer, forcing a groan smothered by his lips. He didn't taste like cinnamon this time. It was saltier from the sweat. "And here I thought your biggest fear was spiders."

I broke free. "You find a spider in my apartment, burn it to the ground."

"Sorry, we didn't fill you in about the club. Theo didn't want to get your hopes up and find out it was a pipe dream." Julian offered us each a hand, pulling us to our feet as if we weighed nothing.

"Surprise," Theo said, wiggling his fingers as he made like he had performed a magic trick.

"I'm sorry I didn't say anything," I confessed. "This is new to me."

"So everybody's sorry? Right? Is this the spot where we have a group hug?" It was easy to see why Theo married Julian. The teleporter liked his men sarcastic.

"No more hugs." I patted my side. "Ribs can't handle it."

"Let's get you to a healer," Theo said, his eyes narrowing as he opened a portal.

"What about the Centurion's base?" I asked. "Should we leave a note?"

"Sorry, we wrecked your cool base. Send me the bill?" Julian turned about, surveying the damage. "Was that his master plan? Property damage?"

"I don't know," I said. "He was convinced he'd won before you got here."

Julian lifted me as if I were a blushing bride. "Priorities. First, we get you fixed. Then we'll talk to the Centurions. Maybe they can shed some light on this disaster."

Theo grinned as Julian cradled me like a stuffed toy. We had just gotten our butts handed to us. We nearly died, and yet he seemed to think it was a riot that his husband carted me around. I shot him a dirty look.

"I didn't say a thing!"

The best part was he didn't need to. Eclipse had thought he could tear me down, and for a while, he did. But in the end, the supervillain's tactics backfired. Now, thanks to some weird telepathic mojo, there wasn't a doubt in my mind about how I fit into this equation. I might have to include that in his eulogy.

We could deal with the ramifications of today at a later time. I needed a doctor to ensure I lived to see another day. After that, I wanted quality time with Theo, maximum body contact, maybe with some popcorn and a rom-com. I wanted to enjoy being the third person in this trio. The rest of the world could wait.

29

———

THE HOUSE SMELLED OF CARNITAS THAT WOULD HAVE MADE my abuela proud. When Julian said he loved Mexican food, I'm not sure he understood what he was getting himself into. There was enough food for an army and easily three days of leftovers. I had ruined them. The local taco joint would never scratch that itch again.

A month had passed since the Nocturnals went on their bender trying to destroy the Centurions. The healer had seen to my wounds, but it still required a week of bed rest. I didn't enjoy being trapped in my apartment, but it gave me time to take notes about the future of Midnight Alley. And I couldn't complain that Theo spent plenty of time resting in bed with me. Everything was better when you had a teddy bear handy.

"Who taught you to cook like that?" Julian asked as he finished loading the dishwasher.

"Grow up in a house of women, and without a doubt, they are going to put you to work. I've shucked more corn than I care to remember."

Theo laughed. "So I can't ask for elote next?"

"Don't make me reach across this couch."

He laughed. When Theo first asked me out, I had been worried about having to share the man with his husband. It required a bit more communication than I was used to, and don't get me started on scheduling. But I hadn't considered the benefits that came with two men. I had cooked dinner while Theo set the table, and now Julian had finished the cleanup. I had gained a relationship and a friend. It was hard to grasp what had terrified me at the start. This was a home I could get used to.

"Can we finally talk business?" asked Julian.

"I'm too full to argue," Theo said, rubbing his belly. "If villains attack, they can have the city."

I searched for my backpack. I crawled to the end of the couch, unzipping the bag and pulling out my notebook. It wasn't a fancy legal binder, but the fact I was writing down ideas was already more managerial than I thought possible.

"I came prepared. I've got a list of ideas I wanted to run by you. Scarlet says she's out of the business, but she's been great about helping me prepare for the re-opening."

Julian wandered over to the couch, laying down so that

his legs draped over Theo's lap. They were a cute couple, and I appreciated that they no longer hid their affection. It was endearing to see Theo rubbing Julian's legs in an absent-minded manner. Even cuter when he leaned in to kiss me, and stole the notebook from my hands.

"Check this out. He was worried about taking over. Do I recall you saying you didn't know what you were doing?" He showed the notebook to Julian. "He has multiple quotes for the upholstery. I think he was lying to us this whole time."

My cheeks burned, but I refused to hide. It wasn't much different from dealing with the vendors for the bar. Except now, I wasn't trying to source alcohol, I was hunting for... well, everything. Without Scarlet, I wouldn't have gotten this far, but I was getting comfortable with the process.

"How do the numbers look?" Julian controlled the finances, and ultimately, he wanted to make sure this remained a smart business investment.

"We're thirteen percent under what we expected. I called in a few favors and strong-armed the floor guy. I think we'll be golden."

"See, now you're talking like a boss," he laughed.

Theo had co-signed the loan that had bought the bar, but he wanted nothing to do with the money. He preferred the 'fun' stuff.

"Entertainment?" asked Theo.

"Got it."

"Promotion?"

"The Centurions are grateful that we saved their base. Bernard has them promoting the event. If there's a person with powers out there, they'll know about the club."

"Handsome date for the opening?" Theo batted his eyelashes.

I rolled my eyes. "I've got my feelers out."

Theo gasped. "I'm hurt."

"If you don't find somebody," Julian added, "I'll go with you."

"Then I guess everything is ready to go."

Theo's bottom lip pushed out as he pouted. "I'm not sure I want the two of you anywhere alone." He held it for a second before the smirk returned. Even through the beard, I could see that one side always sat higher than the other. Did it make him more sexy or adorable? Verdict was out at the moment.

Theo froze as he caught me staring. For all his bravado, he blushed easily. Adorable. No, sexy. Dammit, I couldn't decide.

"I don't know why you were worried about taking over the club. I know Scarlet is helping with specifics. But this is your baby now." Julian wouldn't allow me to avoid the praise he said I deserved. For a man capable of bending steel girders, he didn't have the take-charge attitude of his hero counterpart. He was the opposite, a big softie with muscles as thick as my neck.

I closed the notebook. There were hundreds of ideas to keep Midnight Alley relevant and on the forefront of places heroes spent their downtime. Maybe I had a clue what I was doing? It wasn't long ago that my only worry was identifying the next hero to share my bed. But with Theo, I had a teddy bear to keep me company when I needed it.

"Mind if I steal Theo for a bit? I want to show him something."

Julian swung his legs off Theo's lap before jumping to his feet. "That's my cue for bedtime. I have to be up early for court. What they don't tell you about saving the city is all the paperwork. You stop one man from throwing a school bus off a bridge, and you spend the next three days in court giving testimony."

"It's true," Theo said. "And don't even get me started if the villain crosses state lines. Or the worse, when they claim to be insane. Lawyers love an insanity plea. What sane person straps a nuke to their back and threatens city hall?"

Julian leaned over, about to give Theo a kiss. He hesitated, giving me a side-eye. It was going to take some time to navigate this relationship, but seeing the two of them together and the way Julian made Theo smile, jealousy was the last thing on my mind. Soon as I smirked, Julian kissed his husband.

"Don't forget lunch tomorrow," Julian said. "You're welcome to join us."

The invite warmed my heart. I didn't question its authenticity, but I was happy to bow out. If this was going to work, they needed time to be a couple as well. "Appreciated, but while you're having burgers, I'll be dreaming about burly heroes saving the day."

"I'll have to get their numbers," Julian said with a wink. "Night, gentleman. Don't get yourselves into trouble without me."

Theo gave my thigh a squeeze. As I rested my hand over his, I realized his was more akin to a paw. I caught his gaze, and the intensity in his eyes stirred something deep in my gut. Yes, the infamous playboy Alejandro blushed because a guy was staring at him like he was on the dinner menu. I could hear the playful jabs of the breakfast crew now.

He kissed my forehead. "So what is it you wanted to show me?"

30

It was rare that Vanguard City had a peaceful night. I thanked the gods above that the villain menace stayed at a dull roar tonight. Without the moon, the stars filled the sky, fighting against the light from the streets. It was about as perfect as I could hope for.

Theo stepped through the portal onto the roof of my building. He raised an eyebrow as I took his hand. Pulling him along, I stopped as we reached a telescope. I'd have to thank Sebastian for loaning me the gem of his collection. I'd also have to give Griffin a hard time for dating the only man geekier than him.

"What's this?"

"It's a telescope."

Theo pouted. "You're insufferable. I meant—"

"Just look."

I admired his backside as he leaned down to look through the eyepiece. He waited a moment before looking over his shoulder. "I see a star. Am I missing something?"

"You can't see it yet, but in…" I tried to remember what Sebastian told me. "It'll take forty-three years for the light of that star to reach us."

"I get how light travels." He turned back to the telescope, taking another look. I'm sure he was humoring me, but it gave me a chance to focus on how dry my mouth had gone.

"It's blocked by a small planet. In that shadow…" Just say it, Alejandro. Just. Say. It. "You'll see me falling for you."

Cheesy. I know. That could very well make its way into the hall of fame for the worst one-liner of all time. If he turned now, he'd see my face scrunched up, fighting off the creeping heat. I was thankful for the first minute of him fixed to the telescope, but halfway through the second minute, I worried it was over the top.

"That's one of the stars from the planet we visited?"

"It is. Forty-three light-years away, give or take a day."

Theo stood and turned, reaching out to take my hand. His fingers laced through mine, bringing them to his mouth. He planted gentle kisses on each of my knuckles. With a tug, I pressed against him, his lips brushing against mine. He held my face, refusing to let go. I damn near melted while he took my breath away.

"In that case…" He pressed his forehead against mine as

he whispered. "We have a date in forty-three years to see where we began."

My heart overflowed, threatening to force its way from my chest into my throat, making it difficult to swallow. I wrapped my hands around his torso, hugging him tight enough to force the air from his lungs. "Deal."

"Until then..." He kissed along my jaw, following the stubble along my cheek until he reached my ear. "There are plenty of places I want to explore with you."

His breathing sounded like a roar as his teeth nibbled my earlobe. "Rome. The Outback. I'm sure there are more planets." His voice had dropped to barely a whisper, as if he were sharing secrets. "There's an island in the Atlantic where clothes are only a suggestion."

Naked islands? We'd circle back around to that.

I spun him about, pointing at the roof. I snaked a hand around his waist, resting my head on his shoulder. "That's where I want to do my exploring tonight." His back straightened, but he didn't move. "Naked. I mean, naked. Did I not emphasize the innuendo?"

Non-linear spatial mechanics. As Theo leaned backward, I staggered, falling through one of his portals. I would have cursed his name, but the sight of sand dunes rushing toward me had me whimpering. I fell through another portal, launching me through the neon lights of New York City. As I contemplated a thousand ways to kill him, I shrieked. Another portal opened, sending me flying into the sky above the rooftop. Gravity slowed my ascent. But instead of falling the thirty or forty feet below, another portal opened. Only a few inches, and I landed on a plush king-sized mattress, complete with Theo resting on his side, head propped up by several pillows.

"We need some ground rules." My heart thumped loudly in my ribcage.

I stared at the twinkling stars as my body attempted to make sense of the chaos. Had he just teleported me around the globe? Should I be impressed or pissed? Was this his way of showing off, or would every promise of sex involve me being hurled through time and space? I don't think a safe word was going to cut it.

"I was just going to blow you," I mumbled.

"Too much?" he asked.

"Too much," I confirmed.

With the deft hand of a professional zipper wrangler, he popped the button of my jeans. "Can I make it up to you?" I feigned an angry face, but it was cut short as his fingers grazed the tightness in my pants. If this was the solution for every time he behaved badly, I hoped he would never behave again.

"It's a start."

He climbed over me, lifting my shirt until I pulled it off. The kissing started in the middle of my chest, soft brushes of his lips as he moved his way toward my pants. Before he reached his destination, I could feel the teeth of my zipper as my cock strained. I lifted my ass enough that he pulled my pants down. He slid my underwear off, holding the head of my cock between his lips. Theo knew how to tease, and at this rate, I might come before he touched my cock.

The teasing ended when I grabbed the back of his head and bucked my hips. Theo didn't resist as I wiggled my cock free, sliding it between his lips. I fell backward, arching my back to ensure he swallowed every inch. Greedily, he grabbed my hips, pulling himself down until I could feel the back of his mouth. He didn't move, allowing me the chance to savior the curve of his throat. His nose buried into my groin while my fingers sank into the blanket, threatening to tear the fabric.

His body wretched as his gag reflex responded, but he didn't pull away. A man capable of ignoring *that* was worth keeping around. He shot up onto his knees as he tugged at my pants and underwear. Tossing them to the side, he tore off his shirt and unzipped his pants. Watching him push them around his thighs provided a beautiful image of this sexy bear, hard and eager.

He laid down between my legs, his lips wrapped around the head of my cock. I was about to moan a typical male phrase of encouragement. But before I could moan a "Fuck yeah," something poked at the side of my head. I turned to find his cock protruding from a portal. I laughed at the humor of a stiff penis jabbing me in the ear.

"So it's going to be one of *those* sessions?" I asked.

"Dahmstraight," he said around my cock.

Xander and Griffin mocked my affinity for capes. But I doubt either of them went down on their boyfriends without resorting to a pedestrian sixty-nine. I wrapped a hand around Theo's cock, squeezing it enough to force a moan despite his mouth being full. As I licked the underside of the shaft, I suddenly didn't mind being propelled around the globe, not if this was going to be the result.

He stopped bobbing up and down as I slid the head of his cock into my mouth. It wasn't the best angle, not for vigorous sucking, but at least this way, the event wouldn't end quickly. While I worked to get him into the depths of my throat, I plotted the rest of the things on my bucket list before I made him come.

I don't want to get mushy, but there is something different about sex with somebody you're falling for. Every lick, every stroke, was mixed with the pleasure of now, but coated with thoughts of what's to come. There wasn't a need to cram a lifetime of wants and desires into a single act. We had time. The approaching orgasm would be one of many, and I was already excited for the next.

"Slow down," I gasped. "You're going to make me come."

Theo ignored my protests. He slid up and down the length of my cock, running his tongue under my shaft in a slow, persistent motion. The warmth flowed down my body, pooling in my groin as the tingling turned electric. I resumed sucking him, wanting him in my mouth as I—

I moaned as I lost myself in the waves of pleasure. My toes curled in my sneakers and my legs stiffened as I surrendered to the sensation. Theo slowed, finishing with two long strokes as my cock turned sensitive. He made a bit of a show with the gulp, swallowing every drop of cum. I tried not to howl and alert potential onlookers, but the best I could do was quiet myself to a low growl.

Lifting my head, I glanced down my body to see Theo staring at me with my cock in his mouth. It was damned near picture-perfect. This amazing stud of a man, a hero, continued teasing me even after I had come. I turned my head, ready to return the favor, when his cock disappeared through the portal.

"Not fair." I shot him a look.

He kicked off his shoes and scooted out of his pants. Now naked, he crawled his way up my body, tracing the same course along my torso, kissing gently until he reached my chest. It could be the after-effect of an orgasm, but I wanted nothing more than to spend the night tangled with Theo. I almost laughed as I thought about where our romance had started.

"What are you thinking?"

"You know, I almost turned you down that first night."

"Ouch. Sir, you wound my pride."

"It was a rough day at work. Glad I came to my senses."

I imagined him lying on top of me the first time he saved me. There wouldn't be rest until I got on my knees and worshiped him. But it wasn't the sex or even the chase that left me breathless. Okay, maybe the sex was partly to blame. But the rest was knowing he had carved out a spot in his heart for a sarcastic bartender.

"I wonder what would be different if the taxi driver hadn't gotten the directions wrong? Or what if I went home after the Nagatine? What if..."

He placed a finger on my lips. "I'd have found you."

The sarcastic retorts caught in my chest as my throat closed. I tipped my head back, trying to hide the impending tears. Before Bernard, I couldn't recall the last time I let somebody see me cry. His finger slid along my cheek, wiping them from my eye.

"Saving people is what heroes do." He leaned forward, letting his lips touch mine just enough to call it a kiss. "But it's not always the monsters we need saving from."

"I owe Eclipse," I admitted. "If it wasn't for him, I don't think I'd have confronted my fear of getting involved with a—"

"Stud? Epic burlesque dancer?"

"A married man."

The smile faded from his face, leaving him stoic and almost statuesque. "I can say with confidence that my heart is big enough to love two men."

I wasn't ready to drop the L-word, not yet. A month ago,

I would have laughed at the possibility. But now? This man, without knowing it, opened a door to possibilities I had long thought impossible. Dammit. I wanted to reach that point with Theo.

"Fuck me." Okay, perhaps I needed to work on expressing my emotions with words. But the renewed stiffness from Theo confirmed he spoke my love language. Right now, I wanted this man I... liked? Capital 'L' liked, inside me.

"Yes, sir." The devilish smile returned in abundance.

He rolled me over as if I weighed nothing. Before I could bark another order, I moaned at the feeling of his tongue prepping me for entry. Between his beard grazing the underside of my balls or his tongue licking between my cheeks, I was pretty certain if magicians destroyed reality, I'd die a lucky man. To make sure Theo knew, I pushed back, encouraging his efforts.

I was in heaven and considered closing my eyes and drifting off with his scruff brushing along my skin and his tongue prodding me. The thought vanished as he pulled back, sliding a finger inside. Like a professional, he found the spot that wiped sleep off the table and sent me into a mix of moaning and growling. I nearly begged him to stay when he pulled out. The man moved quickly, getting himself into position. Somebody was eager.

He grabbed onto my hips and pulled back until I was on all fours. He slid his cock down the crack of my ass, continuing his teasing. I pushed backward, making it clear exactly where I wanted him. His fervor had made me hard, which could very well be classified as a superpower on its own.

It started with pressure. He held still, partly teasing and letting me take control of how fast I accepted such a thick cock. Theo's powers weren't his only gift, and I appreciated him letting me set the pace. But honestly, I wanted to feel him draped across my back, holding me, the space between us nothing more than a memory.

The sound from my mouth grew louder, as if his cock turned an internal volume dial. His groin rested against my ass and I gasped at the size of him. The base of his cock thickened in just the right way, making me earn the victory. But as it throbbed, I swore he did it to keep bumping against all the bits that made me want to squeal.

"Want to try something?"

I wanted to shout, 'Yes. Anything. Never take your cock out.' But I just gave him a nod as I squeezed his cock. At least now, I wasn't the only one moaning for the neighbors to hear.

He pulled my legs back before easing my hips forward. I couldn't imagine what non-linear madness—

A hand touched my cock, wrapping around it, thumb spreading the remnants of my last orgasm down the shaft. I would have laughed at the idea of coming again, but having this bear in me was all the inspiration I needed. He moved my cock, leaving me confused.

"What are you—"

Theo pushed back, and I could feel a familiar tightness wrap around the head of my cock. I looked down my torso between my legs to see my cock vanishing into a portal. There are many things I can say I've accomplished in the bedroom, but fucking a man while he plowed me had never crossed my mind. I enjoyed being a burly man, but flexibility was not our strong suit.

"Damn, you're hard," he laughed.

"Fucking and getting fucked by my boyfriend? What did you—"

"Boyfriend?"

Capital L decided this relationship needed a label. I pushed forward hard enough to shove him further down my cock. He buckled over, wrapping a hand around my chest. I had been the meat in a bear sandwich before, but they rarely found their groove. Theo, however, made an excellent top and bottom.

He forced my knees wider, allowing him to slide even deeper. I could hardly focus as he worked the length in and out of my ass. Normally I'd beg for him to stay buried deep, but each time he rocked backward, he slid further down my cock. When he picked up the pace, going from a leisurely fuck to drilling me, I feared my eyes would roll back in my head. When he changed tactics, returning to his long and steady strokes, I feared I'd come and end the ride.

"I'm not going to—"

There was no picking up pace, no erratic strokes, just the long groan as Theo squeezed my chest. Theo had a cock that made it obvious he was coming. It thickened, forcing a slight yelp. The vein along the bottom pulsed with each rope of cum he buried in me. But he wasn't getting off that easily. Yes, pun intended.

With quick jabs, I used his ass to massage that sweet spot in the middle of my shaft. His groans turned to gasps, and I thought he might have to tap out before I finished. He might think if I came now it'd be over for the night, but I fully intended to slide inside him again while I played the part of the big spoon later. I wanted to make sure I spent as much time as possible inside my... boyfriend.

"Come for me," he panted.

Who was I to deny his request?

I quickened my strokes. His cock remained buried, and as I shoved all the way back, he swore, twitching inside me. That was all it took. It wasn't a full-body orgasm this time. Instead, the warmth washed along my back, where he continued holding me. Normally, it'd be a meek load the second time, but Theo was going to be sticky. I damn near collapsed with him on me, with my boyfriend, sprawled over me like a furry blanket.

"I'm going to be sore," he groaned.

His legs were covering the lower half of my body as he rolled onto his side. If he thought he was going to be sore from that, he was going to be in rough shape by morning.

His eyes narrowed as he studied my face. "Dammit." He rolled his eyes. "You're already planning the next time. Don't lie. I can see it in your eyes."

I pressed my chest against his, tasting myself on his lips. "It's a rough life being my boyfriend." He could act innocent all he wanted. But between Julian and me, Theo was going to be exhausted more often than not. He might need to save people on other planets to get some rest.

"You're going to be more trouble than a clone army, aren't you?"

31

Even with the light pollution from the city, the absence of the moon made the stars shimmer. I couldn't find our planet, but as we lay on the blanket, legs tangled together, it was enough knowing it was out there. There might be birds that left streaks of fire in their wake, but I think we did a pretty good job of making a little fire of our own.

Theo's body jerked as he attempted to fight off sleep. After the last couple of days, he had earned a post-sex nap. I scooted closer, resting my head on his shoulder. His arm gave me a squeeze, forcing me to press against his naked flesh. Eventually, we'd have to go inside to a proper bedroom. Maybe in a few minutes. I wasn't done enjoying the warmth of his body in the cool night air.

"Cough."

My body stiffened. No, not *that* part. I lifted my head slowly, as if our visitor wouldn't notice the movement of two naked bears glistening with sweat. I hadn't heard the stairwell door open. Had somebody been up there the entire time? Had we trapped them here while we howled our way through orgasms?

"I said, cough."

Even in the dead of night, I could make out the vigilante. Hellcat had a reputation of swinging from rooftop to rooftop. What are the chances she picked the one with a puddle of men on it?

"Oh, hey there. How's it going?" Smooth. At least in the dead of night, she couldn't see my face turning red. Or could she? What tech did her mask have? Could she see the ultraviolet spectrum? Jesus, right now, my face probably lit up like a Jackson Pollock painting.

"I would rather fight Dr. Vicious than whatever it was I walked in on. Seriously, is the grunting necessary? I'm pretty sure the residents of Vanguard think a drift of pigs were unleashed on the city."

Should I let her finish the rant before I chimed in? I'm all for sex positivity, and hell, a bit of exhibitionism can make for a fun romp. But flaccid on a roof as a masked crusader commented on my technique? Yup, this was mighty awkward. I should probably—

"Wait. A drift?"

"Yeah, a drift." She cocked her head to the side, trying

to figure out the confusion. Beating her head against the end of her staff, she groaned. "A group of pigs is called a drift. Is this what we're talking about?"

I giggled. "I've been in the middle of a drift before."

"Huh? Who's there—" Theo tilted his head back to see an upside-down Hellcat. It was amusing to see the flash of panic as he rolled over, propping himself up on his elbows. He might think this position better than his cock pointing to the heavens, but if Hellcat had watched our tryst, his ass was just as much a source of raunch.

"Can we help you with anything?" Might as well get to the point. I'm betting she's a voyeur, and this was her thing. It would explain perching on the top of buildings. Easier to see into the windows of couples getting it on before bedtime. Even heroes had their kinks.

Her body straightened at the same time the emotion drained from her face. "I came to speak with EO. We need you."

I didn't think anybody other than Julian and I knew his alter ego. I jumped in to cover. "Close, but his name is Theo. I think you have the wrong—"

"Theo? EO? Let's discuss a less obvious alter ego later."

She had a point. It was bad enough that half the heroes of Vanguard walked around with skimpy masks, thinking it provided anonymity. But at the rate they were going, a guy named Marc would change his name to Mark and think himself safe. Somebody needed to teach our powered community the difference between subtle and stupid.

"What's wrong?" Theo asked.

"I'm putting together a team and we need your help." As if on cue, two capes dropped out of the sky. Both Hyperion and Lionheart were newer heroes, but since their appearance, they had made a name for themselves. If Hellcat had convinced these soloists to join her group, she must have a convincing pitch.

Even in the dark of night, Theo's face lit up. It was the offer he had been waiting for since arriving in Vanguard. "About damned time. What took you so long?"

"We would have asked twenty minutes ago, but you appeared busy," Lionheart said. Hyperion snickered at the comment, a sentiment their leader didn't share. Hellcat shook her head before shooting them a look, silencing the powerhouses.

I couldn't help but chuckle. When you're naked as a jaybird in front of three people known for saving the planet, you can only laugh at the situation.

Hyperion and Lionheart couldn't hide their smirks.

"You're a bunch of deviants," I said.

"Yes," she said, "yes, we are. And these deviants are going to save the world."

Where the two men were new to the scene, Hellcat had been around as long as I worked at Midnight Alley. But if this was a world-saving endeavor, her skill with martial arts wasn't going to be enough. I'm not sure if a Galactic Empire's elite guard cared how hard she kicked.

"I don't want to state the obvious, but isn't this a job for the Centurions?"

The tone shifted. Neither man snickered as Hellcat lowered herself to one knee. She lowered her voice to a whisper as she spoke. "The Centurions are the ones we're saving the world from."

One sentence came with a world of questions. The Centurions were known as Earth's greatest heroes. They had saved the planet from apocalyptic events for as long as I could remember. Bernard. What about Bernard? What did this mean for him? Was I going to need to choose between my boyfriend and best friend?

Theo didn't hesitate. "I'm in."

"¡Dios mío!"

32

———————

For the last week, the club had been closed while we upgraded the sound system and had the furniture reupholstered. I wanted a facelift, familiar, but with little touches that transitioned the club from one stage to the next. A grand re-opening had been Bruno's idea, and I ran with it. Despite being closed, every staff member pitched in. Tonight we prayed it paid off.

I still thought of this room as Scarlet's office. Even without her photographs or newspaper articles on the wall, it didn't quite feel like it belonged to me. Any moment, I'd shoot up in bed, drenched in a cold sweat, and realize this had all been a dream. Staring at the floor-length mirror, I almost didn't recognize the suave man staring back at me.

"Damn. I look good."

If mi madre saw me now, she'd be thrilled with her baby. In the reflection, I could see the bouquet of dahlias. Eventually, I'd invite her to Vanguard City for a visit. If I didn't, she'd show up on my door with la chancla in hand, ready to strike me down like a sharpshooter. I might be brave when it came to villains, but nobody stood a chance against Señora Martinez.

"Handsome as always," came Theo's voice. I spun about to see him and Julian in their pressed super suits as they stepped out of a portal. They were a handsome couple on a bad day. Right now, they looked as if they were going to go on a press tour.

"He's not too shabby," Julian said.

"Don't force me to have you removed from my club." I gave Julian a tight hug and kissed Theo.

"He gets sexy when he's bossy," Theo laughed.

"Trust me, I know. Our walls aren't *that* well insulated."

I ignored the banter. It'd spiral out of control and I'd never get out of the office. "You two should be out there with me. This is only happening because of you."

"Nope."

Theo nodded his head to agree with Julian. "We might have provided an opportunity. But you're the one making this happen. Here, you're the hero."

If they made me cry, I was going to be pissed. I swore I wouldn't get worked up. I knew it'd be a battle all night as emotions bubbled to the surface. It was already difficult to keep my heart from working its way into my throat. They came to support me. They might be my anonymous bene-factors, but they stepped back and let me shine. Dammit, I was going to cry.

"Before you get worked up, we have something for you."

Theo reached through a portal and pulled out a package wrapped in silver paper. He thrust it into my hands, excited by whatever was inside. "Guys, you didn't have—"

"Just open it!" Okay, maybe it was Julian who was overly excited.

I tore at the paper to see an empty picture frame. There was a vacant square in the middle and a similar rectangle beneath that. I wasn't sure what to make of the gift. An empty frame?

"I told you he wouldn't get it," Theo said.

"It's for the article they're going to write about you on opening night. The spot beneath that is for the first dollar you make. It's a reminder of where you started."

A knock sounded on the door. With no fanfare, Theo and Julian vanished into a portal, waving as it closed. I'd see them in the club as they played the role of patron. I set the frame down and opened the door to see Bruno in dress pants and a vest. He had insisted on wearing less, but I didn't want it to become the premier sex club for heroes. Perhaps that'd be the next business we opened.

"She's getting restless. If you don't come out, she's going to walk."

"Damn talent," I said as I straightened my tie, rushing out of the room toward the club. With a final turn, I spotted the diva waiting at the door that would lead onto the stage.

"Scarlet," I said. "I was getting ready. Are we being dramatic?"

"Absolutely," she said with a smile. She gave Bruno a slight wave before pointing to the circular window. "See why."

I squeezed passed her in the narrow space and pressed my face against the glass. It didn't seem possible. Not since before the depowering had the club ever come close to being this full. It was standing room only, and if that wasn't enough, the A-list heroes had come. Front and center, Sentinel held a stein of beer along with the other Centurions.

"It's... packed."

"For me, obviously." Scarlet chimed in. When I didn't respond, she grabbed my head, the silk of her gloves scratching against my stubble. "I had a good run here, but it was time for me to go. They're here for the new. They're here because the right person—"

It was heartfelt, but I didn't need a pep talk, not if I was going to avoid more tears. Before she finished, I pushed my way into the club. As I walked up to the stage, the crowd roared and glasses clanked together. Scarlet had built

Midnight Alley, but it was time for me to push her legacy into the future. Learning to look forward had become a new mantra in life.

In the crowd, I spotted heroes that had long since retired their suits. There were those that still protected our street. Peppered between them was a younger generation, the up-and-coming saviors of Vanguard. Staring back at me was the past, present, and future of Midnight Alley.

I approached the microphone, and the room grew quiet, but the energy didn't diminish. Much to the dismay of our pianist, I lifted his martini off the piano and claimed it as my own. "Maldito. I'm not going to bore you with a speech. I don't have words for this. So I'm just going to say..." I raised my glass high into the air. "As long as I stand, the heroes of Vanguard will find haven in Midnight Alley. As somebody who gets kidnapped more often than he should admit, this citizen thanks you."

The crowd roared with laughter. Glasses chimed as people toasted. I swallowed the martini in a single gulp. Sorry, Mr. Piano player, but I needed that.

"Without further ado, the real reason you're all here. For one night only, a former hero to Vanguard, and still my personal champion, Scarlet Drozdov."

Like a queen, she barged onto the stage. The slit up the side of her shimmering dress made a promise that the audience would receive a sensual and sultry performance. Before she stepped foot on the stage, the sound of her humming carried through the club. In true Scarlet fashion, it held an edge of power, and by the time she reached the microphone, the pianist followed her lead. With a slight shove, she pushed me out of the way and took the microphone.

I jumped down, joining the throng of leather suits, masks, and far too many capes. They patted me on the shoulder and congratulated me on a successful opening. Aiden popped up long enough to gather quotes for Revelations. I half expected Damien Vex himself to appear to get the scoop on the club's new ownership.

But it was Bernard hidden underneath his signature cowl that stared me down. I pushed my way through the crowd until we were standing face to face. Between the music and wall-to-wall heroes talking, I couldn't make out his words. He wrapped me in a bear hug, careful not to spill his drink. With his mouth next to my ear, I could make out his whisper.

"I'm proud of you, mi osito."

"Thanks, Papi."

"Go find your man and celebrate."

He slapped my ass hard enough that it'd leave a mark. Some heroes didn't realize their own strength. Bernard, I'm pretty sure, took pride in leaving a paw print on my cheek. Speaking of men touching my butt, EO leaned against the bar, watching me as I pushed my way through the brutes of the superhero community.

When I reached him, he held two shots. Offering me one, he quickly tapped the glass before downing the contents. I recognized the concoction, one of my signature drinks, except the bartender had been a little heavy with the lime.

"Mr. Martinez, I don't have words."

I grabbed the edges of his suit, pressing the length of my body against him. With a kiss, I realized there had been just the right amount of lime in the shot. EO kissed back, holding the back of my head as I bit down on his lip, savoring the taste.

"I have one question." His voice turned quiet, nearly drowned out by Scarlet's crescendo. He rested his hands on my shoulder, swaying to the music as if we were at a middle school dance.

"What might that be?"

"What's next, Mr. Martinez?"

He took my hand, spinning me about. I pressed my back against his chest as we continued rocking back and forth. Scarlet stood on the stage, belting the lyrics to a song I'd never heard. Near the front door, Bruno held up his hand, stopping latecomers from entering and breaking the fire code. Even the breakfast crew mingled with the heroes. Griffin had his phone out, taking as many selfies as possible.

I had it all, friends who cared for me, a job I cherished. For years I lived in the present, putting off all the things that might come down the road. But as Theo rested his head on my shoulder, I was content in the now but excited for what was yet to come.

"I don't know," I said honestly. "But I'm excited to find out."

"You'll have to let me know what you find."

"I won't have to." I kissed his hand before he gave me another squeeze. "You'll be there with me."

"Yes. Yes, I will."

AFTERWORD

I am a gay man obsessed with superheroes. As a kid, I had no role models, and that hasn't changed much as an adult. Because of this, I bringing my relationships, sex life, and love of comics to the forefront in the *Men of Vanguard Series*. The characters in these books reflect personal experiences and themes set against a fictional backdrop.

ABOUT THE AUTHOR

Superheroes stories are at core of Ryder O'Malley's origin story. Refusing to read as a child, everything changed with the first stack of comics. He has always been a fan of forbidden romances within the pages of comics. It should be expected that he'd turn around and start writing his own stories filled with sexy, super, man-on-man action. Ryder's novels draw on his own experiences as a gay man in search of love.

Ryder lives in Charlotte, North Carolina living his happily-ever-after. When he's not writing, he can be found working on book covers (which means he's admiring huskular bears with a little bit of chest hair.)

9 781953 915115